NEW CENTURY, NEW ERA, NEW EXPERIENCES

VIE

STRATTON
—PRESS—
Publishing Life

NEW CENTURY, NEW ERA, NEW EXPERIENCES
Copyright © 2019 **VIE**

All rights reserved. No part of this book may be used or reproduced by any means, graphic, electronic, or mechanical, including photocopying, recording, taping or by information storage and retrieval system without the written permission of the author except in the case of brief quotations embodied in critical articles and reviews.

Stratton Press Publishing
831 N Tatnall Street Suite M #188,
Wilmington, DE 19801
www.stratton-press.com
1-888-323-7009

Because of the dynamic nature of the Internet, any web addresses or links contained in this book may have changed since publication and may no longer be valid. The views expressed in the work are solely those of the author and do not necessarily reflect the views of the publisher, and the publisher hereby disclaims any responsibility for them.

ISBN (Paperback): 978-1-64345-489-4
ISBN (Ebook): 978-1-64345-693-5

Printed in the United States of America

OTHER BOOKS BY VIE

Each one of our books, volumes 1 to 4, takes you on a journey or a trip:

911 Complete Guide to Natural Healing
Destiny of the doG (Volume 1)
Time is Ticking: The Fifth Amendment (Volume 2)
Karma through the Window of Time (Volume 3)
New Century, New Age, New Experiences (Volume 4)

Biomusic Frequency of Sound is a color vibrational balancing CD imprinted of the language of the light and on a sonic base.

Even though nations may agree on a few things, they unite in their determination to maintain their authority rather than submit to the rule of God's Kingdom
—Psalm 2:2

Messiah means to spiritually liberate the human race.

Contents

Introduction 11

An Ultimate Battle for Control 16

Violence, Disillusions, Paranoia 20

Wesley's Investigation 23

When the Awakening Is Happening and the Elite
  Are Bound to Fail 27

The World of the Past No Longer Works 32

We Are Living in a Window of Opportunity 36

The Healers or the Doctors: The Galactic Missionaries ... 38

When Science Made You Lose Spirituality and Harmony ... 43

Control Your Mind to Free Yourself 46

Parallel Universes, Parallel Dimensions,
  and Parallel Lifetimes Exist 48

CHADD's Mission 50

The Zeta Reticulans 57

The Sirians and the Andromedans 62

The Lion People (Sirius A) 63

Andromedans 65

The Arcturians 66

Ayla, a Whistle-Blower: Something Is Going Wrong 68

Pyramids, Human Vibratory States, and Nine 74

The Magic of 432 Hz 75

I Began to Stare 77

The Takeover 79

Freemasonry, Ancient Egypt, the Islamic Destiny, and the Cabal 84

The Modern Day of Healing 90

You Are Put to the Test 93

The Liberation of the Planet 96

When the Pleiadians Are Here to Guide Human Spirituality 98

The Truth Must Come Out 110

A Dark Intrusion:
A Psychopath Wants to Take Over the World! 113

Lab Research in Atlantis 120

The Return of the Teaching of Healing and Love 122

The New Earth 124

Know That You Are True and Supported 126

The Lyran-Sirian High Councils 131

Back in Time...134

It Is a Critical Part…Now...137

Message..141

An Open Communication with Another Realm........................144

The Attempt but It Fell 153

The Algorithm Shift 156

The Meeting with an Honorable Man in My Journey................163

Music of the Sphere and Mortal Space-Time 167

The Berkland Wave 171

This Eclipse Happens Only Every One Hundred Years..............175

Who Are the Anunnaki?..177

The Teleporter Phone Booth...180

Answers in Truth 182

The Honorable Man's Guidance 189

Preface

You are about to embark on the most unusual and spiritual journey.

The Aquarian values of love, brotherhood, unity, and integrity have now replaced the Piscean values of money, power, and control with rigidity, restricted individual freedom, and limited responsibility.

It is now about individuals assuming more power.

We just entered a new era, a new cycle of 25,800 years. The Golden Age is at reach, but you must act and do your part. Before peace there is chaos. It is happening now. The understanding of the medical system, of the cosmos, the actual religion systems, and the understanding of space and matter are being upside down and have a profound effect on the psyche of all people. The world population has lived nourished by lies and the hidden truth. Discoveries are coming forward in religion, medicine, space; many people have put their scientific career on the line to speculate. Many have been, and are still being, killed for reason of depopulation. By drugs, pollution, torture, poison in food and water, etc., many are deprived of freedom for money purposes. The perception is altered, and more and more are driven by curiosity to uncover the hidden truths. We are living the last past of the battle against the fallen angels.

VIE

It is not a religious battle but a financial war, controlled and orchestrated by the dark.

Do your part and watch your thoughts. You are the light and your thoughts create. Create peace and harmony and go back to spiritual beings of light and harmony. Send peace to the world. Stay united and do not let the politicians separate you. Would the Library of Alexandria not be burned, people would have evolved a lot now.

If only the majority of the world would rejoice
Hold your vision and make it happen.

Introduction

This book, volume 4, is part of the series of writings by CHADD and VIE. They are lessons in expanding your mind and opening up consciousness and having you take a trip.

One day, VIE's life changed after the reunion with her blue flame. She entered a world of conspiracy and lies for nine years, but more were to come.

CHADD and VIE are two angels at work sent by the higher government of the world. CHADD is a Baker Acted, drugged ward of the state and holds the keys to the Divine wisdom. He is kept on drugs, sent to one mental hospital to another by the corrupted justice system, disabling his brain's ability to filter information and blocking signals to his consciousness.

VIE as a metaphysical light and vibratory healer is guided to go back to her original essence, the Blessed Virgin Mary, to reconnect with her. She is now here in a different life to see and live the transformation from the age of Pisces to the age of Aquarius. Now she works with vibrational transformation energy and bringing knowledge and the hidden truth to the masses of people.

It is the Armageddon, the end of the game before judgment day, the end of the control. It is the time when the elite will be overthrown.

The elite are the dynasties, the families of wealth and privilege, and those in control since the dawn of civilization that worship Lucifer.

They came back to guide and inform you with the real information. It is the time of awakening and remembering. They see many, many humans looking for mental clarity, to release stress, emotions, asking for spiritual growth with no idea where to begin with, or how to get there. People have been misguided by the institutions, religions, and churches, and it is sad. But the world is living the last final battle between God and the governments, a world prison system by the government.

It's a system where law and money are integrated in order to bind the world population by and in that system. It's a world prison created in order to train that population to willingly consent to voluntarily bind themselves—to be essentially bonded servants to that system in order to become the mechanism by which the resources, the wealth of the world, which come from all the natural resources, to be the mechanism to harvest that reach the resources, to build out the global civilization that we live in today.

It is a continuum of secret societies and esoteric schools back to the Egyptian, Babylonian, pre-Roman, and Roman time that trained the elite and the bloodlines. The goal is to train them in a belief system, and there are myriads of belief systems, but there is one primary belief system—the belief that control survival. Fear is an energy and an emotion. It has to do with the disconnection from the heart chakra to the emotional energy vortex, the solar plexus.

All law fundamentally is contract; it means people must voluntarily consent to an agreement that willingly endorses beings' participation.

But the world is at a turning point, a bifurcation that requires every individual to make a choice at that point. The earth is ascending and separating in two. You must make a choice now to continue to be bound in the bounded and continue with the old earth or choose freedom and ascension with the new one.

There are two ways of teaching: one is the light and the other is darkness. Between those two ways, there is a vast difference because posted over one are the light-bearing angels of God, and over the

NEW CENTURY, NEW AGE, NEW EXPERIENCES

other, Satan; one is the Lord from all eternity to all eternity while the other stands as controller over this present age of iniquity.

The first way is the path of light to aid your steps on the road, and illumination has been given to all. Love your Creator; fear Him and give glory to Him who redeemed you from death. Practice singleness of heart and a richness of the spirit. Shun the company of those who walk in the way of death. Abhor anything that is displeasing to God, and detest every form of hypocrisy. Do not cast covetous eyes on a neighbor's possession. Do not be greedy for gain. Do not set your heart on being intimate with the great, but look instead for the company of people who are humble and virtuous. Give your neighbor a share of all you have, and do not call anything your own. Don't be those who stretch out hands to take, but draw back when the time comes from giving. Cherish as the apple of your eye anyone who expounds the word of the Lord to you. Never hesitate to give; when you are given, do it without grumbling and you will soon find out Who can be generous with His rewards.

The second way is that path of the Dark Lord (Satan/Lucifer), which is devious and fraught with damnation. It is the way to eternal death and punishment. It destroys the souls of men: idol worship; brazen self-assertion and the arrogance of power; adultery, cant, and duplicity; manslaughter and robbery; vanity, rascality, sharp practice, spitefulness, and contumacy; sorcery and black magic; greed; and defiance of God. They persecute the virtuous; they hate truth and love falsehood. They know nothing of the rewards of righteousness or devotion to goodness and just judgment. Gentleness and patience are altogether alien to them, and all they care for is paltry and worthless. All they look for is their own advantage. They have no pity for the poor, nor ever trouble their heads about any poor soul in distress. They are always ready with malicious rumors, for knowledge of their Creator is not in them. They make away with infants, destroying the image of God, and they turn the needy from their doors. They deal harshly with the afflicted while they aid and abet the rich; they are brutal in their judgement of the poor. They are utterly and altogether sunk in sin.

VIE

CHADD and VIE came back again to help, as they did during the Egyptian time and Atlantis. They still cared for the world and came to help with the last battle. They are confronted with many trials and contributions in their separate journeys and different life events.

While CHADD is under the MK control program and sent away from VIE in Chateau Asylum, the world continues to go in chaos.

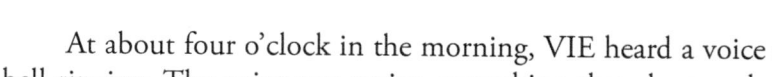

At about four o'clock in the morning, VIE heard a voice and a bell ringing. The voice was saying something that she translated in "Wake up, begin the breath of light, *equalize*. Now go to your space and be. You have now access to all information."

NSA's illegal surveillance techniques linked to public. WikiLeaks. Cabal can't shoot Red Cross workers. Police, FBI, CIA exposed. FEMA preparing for twenty million deaths. Corruption everywhere. Governments gone out of its way.to create incidents but come as savior, appearing as protecting but only for 1 percent of truth to population. What people don't realize is they put their own children in danger. Satanic rituals in courtrooms. Trafficking of human organs. Extreme violence in the streets of Mexico. Russian Mafia. The defending of the Constitution a lie. People put in deep hypnosis coma from nine to ten months, program into that individual a sort of second split personality, have filled knowledge one sort of existence to other. Other world no visible light. HAARP managing ionosphere, with small pieces of aluminum. Anonymous military.

Thoughts appeared, followed by visions. First, brilliant spots of white light of different geometrical forms appeared. Then instead of memories of long time forgotten, people appeared ghostlike in her mind's eyes, processing in sequence, one after the other. She remembered having such experiences while in Costa Rica. Long nights spent in wakefulness, face-to-face with people with whom she carried long conversations. VIE sees Anabelle, a Catholic archbishop Fulton Sheen who wants to be called bishop, Catholic and Tibetan

NEW CENTURY, NEW AGE, NEW EXPERIENCES

monks, priests, archangels, saints, and finally someone from a faraway star in the cosmos. This was the beginning of a series of visions and conversations with them that she provides below. Please open up yourself. Do not judge. Just allow yourself to feel it with your intuition.

In the beginning was the word, the word was with God, and the word is God.

An Ultimate Battle for Control

As the chosen Aquarius in this new Aquarius era, I am totally guided into this writing by my helper from Zeta Reticuli.

In the early stage of the Aquarius era, one humanoid reptilian woman, part of the cabal and in a political power role, said that deep-seated cultural codes, religious beliefs, and structural biases had to be changed. We have to finish it once and for all, she said. Really!

The influential politician woman worshipping Lucifer hypnotized people into manipulating their mind and their clear thinking. She killed many innocents for power and money. She was involved in sex orgies, child trafficking for sex, and has no shame or remorse. She has no feeling. She is simply diabolic and is at the service of satanic entities. Humans need to understand the forces behind this global conspiracy that operates in the shadow. Why do they want the children's energy, and why throughout history people have talked about sacrificing young virgins to the gods?

These reptilians are known as archons in gnostic writings and the djinns by the Islamists. These entities feed themselves on human energy. The energy of different frequencies syncs with other energies of different frequencies, and these entities absorb human energy that is within the frequency range that they can absorb. This relates to low vibrational human emotions, and it relates to fear, to frustration, and to depression. The motion that leads to violence is in wars, conflicts, and individual collective are all energy that they absorb. There is a particular energy that they delight in, which is the energy of children before puberty.

At puberty, a hormonal chemical change happens when children are moving into adulthood. This is the energy that these entities want to absorb as food. It is a power source for them and, for that reason, has happened throughout history. It refers to the sacrifices of children to the gods. A very large number of these children that disappear end up in sacrificial rituals as sacrifices. Pedophilia is always linked to these top people of the society, the major bloodline personalities.

Children end up also as pedophiles and have their energy vampire. During the process of the energy of the child being released, the satanic entities absorb its energy. These reptilians' bloodlines were known in the ancient world as demigods and are hybrid genetic creations that are part human and part reptilian. It is said that when a pedophile of this bloodline is having sex with a child, the entity possessing that pedophile and stimulating that desire for sex with children is drawing off the child energy through the Satanist at the pedophile and absorbing the child energy.

This fact cannot be approached with a religious, political, or scientific belief or you will never understand and awaken to what is going on in the world. You will censor or rebuke the information that media has hidden to you for years. Pedophilia, Satanism, and the establishment is important so human beings can connect the dots.

They were created specifically to be the middle men and women to represent the agenda of these hidden entities in human society. Often human beings are manipulated and have their society directed by forces they do not know exist because that is done by people of influence and in power, key places that look like human and are conduits.

These hybrid bloodlines were created so that they could be very powerfully possessed by these entities mentally and emotionally and could be taken over. They are just entities on earth to manipulate human society while humans have no idea that they exist.

VIE

The humanoid reptilian woman, a hybrid, referred to a battle that began a long time ago.

From the early Christianity writing by Ignatius, whose other name is Teophorus, there is a personal and moving written letter. The author of the book says, "After ages this became the most popular and widely quoted of all the Ignatian writings; its influence on persecuted Christians everywhere was enormous, and it took permanent rank as a kind of 'martyrs' manual."

Ignatius writes, "For the work we have to do is no affair of persuasive speaking; Christianity lies in achieving greatness in the face of world's hatred… All the ends of earth, all the kingdoms of the world would be no benefit to me: so far as I am concerned, to die in Jesus-Christ is better than to be monarch of earth's widest bonds. He who died for us is all I seek; He who rose again for us is my whole desire… Do not have Jesus-Christ on your lips, and the world in your heart… There is no pleasure for me in any meats that persist, or in the delights of this life; I am fain for the bread of God, even the flesh of Jesus-Christ, who is the seed of David; and for my drink I crave that blood of His which is love imperishable."

A long time ago, a Christian sect saw a definite battle of love and materialism in the world of their days, something that has gotten even more defined. That group was known as the Cathari throughout history, its roots in Jerusalem soon after Christ was crucified.

The Cathari realized the end of their days was quickly approaching since the Persians were continuously sacking the city. They were considered heretics by the Roman Catholic Church.

They believed in a God of good and a God of evil. For them, love and power were completely incompatible and matter was seen as a manifestation of power, which was also incompatible with love.

The Cathari believed that Jesus has been a manifestation of spirit unbounded by the limitation of matter, a sort of Divine spirit or feelings manifesting within humans. They proclaimed that the God of the Old Testament was really the devil. They also believed that there was a higher God, the true God, and Jesus was described as being that true God or His messenger.

NEW CENTURY, NEW AGE, NEW EXPERIENCES

Besides the New Testament, the three sacred texts to the Cathari were the *Gospel of the Secret Supper*, or *John's Interrogation*, the *Book of the Two Principles*, and the *Book of Enoch*. The God found in the Old Testament had nothing to do with love known to the Cathari. The Old Testament had created the world as a prison and demanded from the "prisoners" fearful obedience and worship. This God was the God worshipped by the Roman Catholics.

As at the epoch of the Cathari, at this Aquarius era, human beings on earth are prosecuted, tortured, and killed the same way by the Cabal.

Dinosaurs were human beings like us and were killed by the advent of a rock 6,500 years ago that hit the earth, but not of all them. Some of them could not stand the light and went to live underground and advanced themselves and survived.

Evolution is a fact for every creature, and they became scientific, from reptile to one time the group evolved to human forms. They are very advanced but they lack feelings.

They became creatures that now want to control the planet. This is part of the UFO that can be seen. Not all but they control one particular UFO. They can shapeshift. They do not come from another planet and do not want human beings anymore.

There is more than a war between Syria, Afghanistan, and other countries; their purpose is to kill as many human beings as possible.

Their planet is based on evil, and it is time that people realize it. People have to stop thinking that they are coming from another planet, from the cosmos and are looking like humans.

The Illuminades, the Cabal, know the power of appearance. They look like humans, they shapeshift, and human beings must be aware of it. Notice that it's happening on an international level. It is a global network.

Violence, Disillusions, Paranoia

CHADD finally reached his limit. He could not take it anymore. His mind was in a constant foggy state. Taking all these drugs affected its ability to think and function normally. The Father instructed him to go and look for something with copper.

He found VIE. Could it be that the two of them had found each other once again across time, space, and continuum? "I have been reconnected and you got me at Yoap!" she said. This was enough for both to understand. They knew that they were here to accomplish their galactic mission.

CHADD had been arrested for burning candles to our Lady of Guadalupe and other saints while reading the Bible and praying by the window! Really? Nineteen months later, he was still in a state hospital, but no lawyers had been able to locate him in the system or find any case to defend!

So they asked him to read a document of a fake police report in front of a camera to raise a case against him.

While on meds, the CIA applied their ultimate mind control technique. This was a code name that was given to an illegal program of experiments on human subjects.

NEW CENTURY, NEW AGE, NEW EXPERIENCES

It starts when the subject is very young, around five to six years old. It involves chemical drugs, torture, sleep deprivation, hypnosis, amnesia, mind control, and sonic technology to control consciousness, creating trauma and resulting in a split personality. They are put in psychotropic drugs, then the split personality can be programmed for the CIA agents to perform assassinations, blackmail, and espionage.

They experiment on unsuspecting people, a government-founded CIA operation aimed to investigate on how the human mind could be controlled through various means.

They are all part of the Cabal. Through wars and disease, the reptilians want earth people to die. They do not want anyone to know where you go when you are going to die. Dying is graduating.

Heaven and hell exist, but not in the way the religions teach you. Heaven describes a higher level of dimension and hell describes the lower realm. At this beginning of the new era, the actual Aquarius time, humans are living on the planet in the lower realm.

The human body is a sort of organic machinery for all souls. Earth has a magnet artificially created by the reptilians to entrap human souls. The human soul is a source of energy for the Cabal to power themselves, to power their machine. They torture and kill and feed out of your energy. Many human beings also disappeared, vanished, and died for that purpose.

It is not about karma and reincarnation but a net that reptilians use to keep you in a game you can't get out of. You are trapped in a loop and just circle around and around.

There is a council of thirteen, the new world order or new world elite, all claiming to be descendants of the God of the world. Through their created industries, politicians and the newspeople are just actors. Their journalists and reporters read a text; they all read the same script to satisfy the elite, only what they are allowed. They all have to report the same story.

What they do is trap you out of reality, causing wars or creating conflicts by making you believe. They implant it in your brain, and the human brain then creates the image, and conflicts arise.

VIE

I controlled my frustration and decided to call my cousin Jean and asked him if I could visit him in Miami for the weekend. He was effectively going to be in Miami with his wife, Chloe; they were having friends for the weekend. I packed a few clothes, got in my car, and went to the airport.

I landed just in time for dinner. Jean came alone to pick me up at the airport, and I rapidly told him my concern.

"Let's call my friend Alex tomorrow," said Jean. "He owes me a big favor. He should be able to reach Wesley."

The following morning, we went to a chain coffee shop at the nearest corner and we both ordered a cappuccino and a croissant.

I was coming to the table carrying the orders to hear Alex saying on the phone, "We must have this known globally by the media. We can't keep it for us, and we cannot take a chance to have this hidden once more. Enough is enough. It is spreading around the world, and the population has no idea of what these politicians are doing for money purposes." I saw that Alex was carrying with him some documents in a file. Before I asked him what it was, he answered my curiosity. "We must mail these documents overnight to him when we are finished. I have everything documented here. I am glad that you came to visit and discuss it with me. I was working on it for a little while now."

Wesley's Investigation

Wesley made the investigation. He started from what VIE told him about this alien man that stared at her at the gas station and seemed to have no soul, no feeling, and no expression, not human. Wesley discovered how they manipulated CHADD's actions to arrest him each time. They poisoned and unbalanced his body more than ever. They injected him with some psychotropic chemical drugs, which was a nanochip. This was initiated through a program they set up called MK-Ultra.

They provided him from the earliest age with electromagnet poison and disruption that knocked his body optimum balance way out of order. They did so to make the subject react mentally, emotionally, and physically exactly as they planned. They wanted as little opposition as possible while proceeding toward their ultimate goal.

MK-Ultra was for a secret CIA mind control program. Its purpose was to perfect a truth drug for interrogating suspected spies through hypnosis and primitive drug research. It began focusing on the identification and testing of psychotropic drugs in interrogations and the recruitment of agents. The research included laboratory experiments on both animal and human subjects.

Later the CIA's Office of Scientific Intelligence continued it under the name Project Siala, its first mind control program to learn how to condition subjects to withstand information from being extracted from them by interrogation methods to exert control. They developed memory enhancement techniques and established ways to prevent hostile control of agency personnel.

Then it was renamed Project Thistle, then MK-Ultra under deputy and director Ronald Hugues. It aimed to control human behavior through psychedelic and hallucinogenic drugs, paramilitary techniques, and psychological/sociological/anthropological methods, among others. An open field of mind experimentation tried anything that might work, legal or otherwise, on willing and unwitting subjects.

Everything top secret and recorded later on was destroyed—thousands of pages with documented evidence of the horrific experiments and their effects on human subjects. Unwitting guinea pigs suffered hallucinations, memory loss, incoherence, and severe personality changes.

The Illuminati council of thirteen was made of global elite families from around the world and a tiny handful of billionaires secretly ruling and oppressing the world and CHADD. Their system is based on the Egyptian-Babylonian mystery religions. The priestly class reports to the satanic bloodline. The power behind them is clearly nonhuman. They are the fallen angels. Their elite control politics, world army, money, justice—everything. They are the one that brought the terrorist Muslims, to let them make horrible terrorism acts. Muslims to invoke terrorist acts on the population and say, we will kick them out the country.

Germany runs Europeans to fold it into one government. People are hypnotized and asleep, unable to see the reality, and some are under "remote neural monitoring mind control technology."

The human body is a vibratory and an electromagnetic organism, and as such, each organ in your body vibrates at a different frequency of electromagnetic frequency. CIA and NSA targeted CHADD with mind control technology using either satellites or land-based, fixed, phased array of scalar wave towers in the US, controlling him day or night but primarily in its sleep. The CIA agent locked onto its brain wave signal after they moved close to him and trained its brain to their remote neural monitoring system, downloading its specific brain wave frequency, brain wave pattern, into their computer. CIA and NSA handler whistle-blowers, usually four to six handlers, operated in shifts and mimicked by inducing all kinds of thought, emotions, cognitive abilities, physical sensations, etc. They also tracked him with implants. They then locked onto his brain wave pattern frequency and used him.

VIE was next to him, several times, but because of the frequency of directed energy specifically tuned on CHADD, she was just an observer. VIE's brain waves did not operate along the same frequency. This was how they could target one person as the crowd of people didn't absorb the energy or feel its effect. Once they had CHADD's frequency, they could use him from great distances with their mind control technology. However, verification was necessary, and they needed to be close to him or have hidden cameras up or boots on the ground to monitor him and make sure the technology was working.

They sent several aliens to telepathically direct his acts when he washed the car with a pink soap and did not care if VIE would be left responsible for her rental car damaged. They sent their aliens several times to the Mercy Chapel parking lot on several occasions. They used his brain to make a phone call to 911 from the chapel, when he insulted the priest or asked the priest to find him companionship. They made him drive at high-speed limits all over downtown, made him run red lights by taking control of his brain and the car, and sent some alien policemen to arrest him. These aliens had no expression or human emotions. They used CHADD like they were spreading chaos to justify the police point.

Then came the time of intimidation, and twice they tried to eliminate the God duo by accident. The first time they used a veteran with an eighteen-wheeler truck to back up to their car; another time, CHADD grabbed the steering wheel while VIE was driving. They were expecting the accident to happen that the firefighters were already on location before it happened and had already blocked the traffic.

VIE

But VIE as a warrior of God did not let negativity spread into the world, and she encourages you to do the same, using the "Lord's Prayer" and she also says, "The mind is a powerful tool to use, and I keep invoking and calling for the activation of the Violet Flame Grid of Light and Protection and for the White Light upon the entire planet. The Violet Flame is the masculine aspect of the seventh ray and has important qualities. It transmutes negativity and also protects you in that it has the ability to make you invisible to lower vibration and intentions of harm.

"The Grid of Light can be called to form around your own body, your home or office, your car, your loved ones, and your coworkers. You can send this protection to anyone anywhere in the world because distance does not affect its potency. You can visualize that your loved ones receive it and that it is spiraling and spinning around their body.

"This is an important tool, which benefits you, others, and Mother Earth. It protects your home and your personal environment and helps alleviate harmful energies from earth and all humankind as it clears the environment of earth and all five elements."

When the Awakening Is Happening and the Elite Are Bound to Fail

"A chill went up my spine as a flask of lightning revealed to me that your children go from the womb to programming at school. They are put on tiny boxes under surveillance, like me," said CHADD.

I stood there looking at the vision, unable to stop it. This world is an all collective reality and an illusionary reality. It is a world that we see existing outside of us and that is in reality in our brain and goes in a cycle. It's a loop. It turns around and comes back but not exactly the same. It is a version of time that is an illusion and it is all about limitation.

The world is living a period of hidden truth that is now unhidden. The awakening is happening.

The elite, the cabal, does not want to be exposed to the light. They are terrified by the idea and are more and more extreme to stop what is unfolding. The awakening is in the world, though they knew this was coming.

Their system is based on the Egyptian-Babylonian mystery religions. The priestly class reports to the satanic bloodline. The power behind it is nonhuman; they are the fallen angels. Human lives are orchestrated and led by the Anunnaki from Niburu.

VIE

It is tiny elite that controls politics, the world army, banking systems, and money. They are rewiring the population's brains through smartphones.

They are against the vibrational change that can't be stopped until they stop, attack, and limit more and more people. They are throwing everything they can to stop the change.

They are in a hurry to reduce the population and modify the planet. With junk food that is addictive, vaccines weaken the children's immune system for life because of dangerous additives in the vaccines that engender terrible side effects. It systematically targets the body, and people who eat junk food will never be healthy in their life. Drugs are poison to the body and addictive to the DNA. Water is a human right, but we have to pay for it, they keep it away from us, and it is polluted. It contains drugs, chemicals, fluoride, and many more things that endanger human life. They manipulate the weather and justify it by global weather. Jet streams are devastating to farmers. They use all these as a weapon of wars, getting people out of their land by overflow rainful of chemicals. They cause earthquakes and created robots that take the power away, and the journalists are manipulating the people by spreading lies and programming the population with their lies.

There is chaos and the cabal has created a sense of dividing to justify the police point. They bring radical Muslims all over the world then say that they are going to fight them and kick them out of the country.

All humans are a piece of the puzzle here in this journey together to awaken from amnesia. There is a need to wake up and pay attention. The ignorance makes you a sheep. Three years from today, only one out of seven is ready to ascend. When there is discrepancy between beliefs and behaviors, something must change to eliminate or reduce the dissonance.

The human is a holographic body of light, an electrochemical organism balanced to decode all the time. The universe that you experience is a wave of vibrational information construct and the physical. The holograph is like a movie screen, and the wave form level, or the metaphysical universe, is a kind of projector in a move theater. What happens is that the human body computer is decoding that metaphysical universe information into a holographic reality on the human screen, decoded by the brain. But it actually looks right now like an infected computer with a virus as the low vibration knocks out the body system.

The body is made of 85 percent water. The moon influences life on earth and the water. The moon also has influences on the human body and its hormonal system. It breaks out of the five senses reality. Women of all ages experience it through bleeding, some for a couple of day and others up to fifteen days.

But the energy, the correct vibration of the new epoch, is going to be the dominant one. People are awakening and the elites are bound to fall. We are breaking out of their control. This is going to happen.

Though a lot are refusing to see the truth and move. The basic of frequency range, only if you allow and accept it, you will then adjust to see the right frequency. Everyone is equal in this mission.

The reptilians, archons, greys, the elite, the cabal, the enluminades, the illuminati are very intelligent, but they are spiritually dead and totally insensitive. Humans are more spiritual, but the reptilians suppress them by their technology. For these dark energies, their technology is their God. Reptilians are holding back humans so that they cannot grow. But humans have the creative ability that archons don't have. Archons can only change twist or bend the reality.

Humans are more spiritually evolved than reptiles but suppressed by technology that is turning humans into a fake reality by manipulation of human genetics.

They decided to create a man like the image of their God and our likeness that will become a vehicle for them. The computer is information on life in the planet, and it tells them how human life is going to be transformed.

Reptilians' bloodlines and Hollywood worship a secret society. These archonic forces, the elite hybrid, have a particular DNA and a different low frequency than normal human beings. They interbreed to hold the information field and have the ability to delete empathy, remorse, and shame. They are parasites to the society and liars. The reptilians and archons can possess and control humans because of their low frequency and their point of light at the heart center is not visible anymore.

Planet earth has been infiltrated by these hybrids that can shapeshift—like the harsh woman also called the surrogate that kept CHADD in a loop and in limitation of life because of forced ingestions of repetitive psychotropic prescription. And with other human beings in states hospitals, asylums, and behavioral places, they take human form thinking to bring their own reality by using their own low frequency. They kept CHADD under camera surveillance to observe his reaction under drugs, while making money. Carolina, the social worker for money purposes, bed for purpose, convinced the judge to arrest him. He was going to be released by Mrs. Oshtein, but the harsh archon woman found out and had Oshtein replaced by Dr. Kleecase, who tried to persuade him to recognize and sign some fake documents containing false allegations to justify his arrest. This would let them keep him longer and, once released, be able to bring him back again and again.

All information is holographic and must be tuned in through remote viewing. Remote viewing is a feeling in the heart, then you move to the field of information to access.

But humans stop communicating with time and space when they are disconnected. They cannot experience the reality outside time and space. It is the way the reptilians are controlling people in a loop, by taking off the point of interacting with the world. Humans have been disconnected from the point of heart into the emotions. We see how people today react from this point of emotions instead of the point of heart with stress and fears, and if you add drugs, you lack clarity in the mind. Humans then become an easy prey to be possessed. Drugs are demons. They then take possession of the brain to govern your perception. The idea is to pull people to the lowest level.

It is why it is very important that you understand that you are under their dominant manipulation. They are ISIS. They are the terrorists.

NEW CENTURY, NEW AGE, NEW EXPERIENCES

But humanity can defeat easily the dark forces by uniting together. It is time to change from indoctrination to education to raise consciousness.

This era is about defeating the European Union's centralized dictatorship.

The World of the Past No Longer Works

Something occurred at that point, shifting my awareness. I looked up at the stars; this glance triggered a recollection of something extraordinary. I was excited when I began to remember all my past knowledge from previous lives.

Now I can tell you for a fact that you are living in a world where something is wrong. Humanity has reached the point where unstainable ways of thinking and living have caught up with them and science is telling them that human life is not random!

Civilization is cyclical. We just moved from Pisces to Aquarius. You are not victims of this world. You do not have to suffer, live in disease, in poverty, or grow old like science tells you. It is not necessary to use wars to solve the problems. You are living the time where altogether is happening right now. The field of energy exists. That is a fact, and every one of you is participating and speaks to this field.

Tesla said, "If you want to learn about the world, think frequency, energy, and vibration."

Sometimes science is wrong. What you are thought is now obsolete and false. The truth is that earth's magnetic field has effects on human DNA. Human emotions affect the DNA, and prayers are very powerful.

NEW CENTURY, NEW AGE, NEW EXPERIENCES

There is something in the field that gives you the power to heal your body but also can and will bring peace in the world when you understand its language and how to speak to it. You have been told that your inner heart's experiences and thoughts, your emotions, feelings in your bodies, and your prayers have no effects to the realization of your will from invisible to visible. It is false.

You must start working now with your love and your heart. The feeling in your heart is a powerful language. It does not happen in your mind but in your heart, and modern science finally began to understand it has a direct effect on the world.

You are powerful human beings able to change the world and your lives. You must believe. Miracles are beliefs and belief is the code of possibilities. You are part of the universe and you are cocreators. You cocreate it. Your consciousness is creating the universe, but you live your lives based upon your beliefs that come from what science, religion, family, friends, school, the media, TV, and reporters tell you! You are living the life on other people's thinking that are incorrect.

You have been maintained in the dark and afraid of your own power to heal and what you are creating in this world. You are afraid of the power within you to heal the suffering on a subconscious level.

It is the science that children are going to use to solve the problems today. It is a very different way of thinking about things.

There is no stronger force than when you are working with your love and your heart. It is when you envelop yourselves in a white light and allow the white light to run through your physical body and to shield you and, using unconditional love, send your love from you heart to another heart chakra. You do this to diffuse those dark energies and their power and to empower those positive ones to become more powerful.

The human body is made of quantum physical energy that can do miraculous things. It can exist in one place in a moment in time or two or many places at the same time, and they are always connected with one another and can communicate with themselves in the past and in the future. You can do what these particles can do, based on what you believe to be true. What you believe in your heart, you can change into present. The particle can be changed in the past, even when the past already happened. As an intuitive and metaphysical healer, I have done that many times and guided others to do it for healing purposes.

You are made of particles that show you your possibilities. It translates the field into reality. In the field of possibilities everything already exists—peace, joy, healing. With your mind, you reach in those possibilities; you just have to imagine your healing, the peace in the world, your abundance in your life, and trust in the process. With your heart, you breathe into it.

Belief is the union of thoughts and emotions. Thoughts happen in the upper chakra (a chakra is a wheel of energy), and emotions happen in the lower chakra. Feeling is the union of emotions, and thoughts and feelings happen in your heart. Atoms look like waves of energy not like they have been described as a form. To change an atom, you must change the energy. When you change the electric field motor the magnetic field, you change the atom.

Now the heart has a magnetic resonance field, and it produces the strongest magnetic field in the body. It is where you have the feelings, and it actually creates waves of electrical and magnetic energy in your body. That is what the ancient knew and left in temples, ancient texts, and monasteries in Tibet, Egypt, and Peru. Collective prayers have physical healing power.

The heart produces the field that changes your life—what you believe of your body, your lives, and the world. What is happening in the world is creating what is happening actually.

Beliefs change your physical world. Beliefs change the world.

Now you understand why the elite of the world that control you do not want you to know the truth. Now you understand why they have hidden the truth to you by lying to you, by destroying, changing, and twisting ancient knowledge.

This is why the reptilians are terrified by the idea of you learning the truth. They have implanted in you false information for years. They will no more be able to kill, create wars, and feed themselves on human beings' low energy on which they feed themselves.

The actual world is a like a still wave that pulses but does not move. Atoms are stationary. Quantum possibilities are the waves that are moving, going, and coming. It is your heart that locks the quantum possibilities into the reality at this moment.

The global word changes, and when the world changes, it always brings weather changes.

Frequency of Sound CD by VIE is a very powerful healing tool to help you reach your goal and be realigned with your path. It's through the energy of love that all is achieved, like healing.

You are not responsible for global warming, and because it has already happened in the past, the satanic cycle is driving back the past. It affects the hormonal system, ovulation cycle, your heart rate, neurons, and the social cycle.

Watch out over your thoughts because you as humans are the extension of thoughts. What you believe of you lives; your body is what is happening in your world. Beliefs change your physical world. They change matter. This is why you also have the responsibility to only create the best for everyone involved.

There are two types of reptilians—the benevolent that never step on your freewill and the others that want to control the earth. The archonians are known as Isis on earth. They implant viruses, and you need to protect yourself and keep the light around the planet while all of this is going on.

There are one hundred thousand star seeds all over the planet that are helping you.

Stay united and pray together.

"Again I say to you that if two of you agree on earth concerning anything that they ask, it will be done for them by My Father in heaven. For where two or three are gathered together in My name, I am there in the midst of them" (Matt. 18:19–20).

WE ARE LIVING IN A WINDOW OF OPPORTUNITY

I stepped out of the restaurant and heard a male voice talking to me. I turn myself to see who it was coming from and felt this disturbing energy. I continued walking toward my car, and the man followed me. I finally told him that I was in a hurry and had to go, that I did not have the time to socialize right now. Besides, I did not have the intention to. I hurried in my car and locked myself in. The man passed the car, and that's when I saw his transformation and all I could see was this very long and furry brown wolflike tail. I looked at the wall in front of me down the road on a building. On it was written in big letters "Jesus." I was so happy to read the Christ's name and felt the sense of protection over me.

That is when I heard, *As long as we stay in our lives in unconditional love, it does not matter what being we meet or see. We will still maintain our power. We are going to have more of the dark coming on earth, but humans have greater power then they do.*

We live in the Christ consciousness and we live in love, and there is no greater power than that. When you come to earth, you choose what lesson you need to make you stronger. Sometimes, it also happens the lesson is so hard that some of you can't handle it and have to live that earth.

NEW CENTURY, NEW AGE, NEW EXPERIENCES

We, CHADD and VIE, are disliked by the elite. They fear our power when we are together because we have an energy exchange at the heart center. Imagine, the heart is the most powerful weapon that exists! We represent their highest fear, so they arrested CHADD to separate us. Our separation does not exist though; the heart exchange is still there. And we have the key to the book of knowledge.

So what they did was bending our reality. They first poisoned him as a warning, cut his Achilles tendons, then beat him several times and drugged him, then used him in many different ways. But they are frustrated he has so much love for humanity, he never stole or hurt anyone, though they tried hard. He never fought back but with a smile.

I surrounded myself with the white light and the Violet Flame Grid of Light of protection and transformation and projected myself to the past, right where our path was unbent yet, and wired it to the present and locked it, then sealed it.

With a period of a little more than fifteen years of battle to detox CHADD from the drugs that he was forced to ingest, he is having signs again of incontinence, and the system is to be blamed for. But I asked a group of doctors from our spiritual family on another realm to help him. I just needed to vocalize my need and say it aloud. My intent actually was pure enough.

People want to be like us and some are jealous, but we are the chosen one and people have to realize that there is a great deal of work and sacrifice. We have to work constantly and have our consciousness focused all the time.

Would you think to be jealous of Jesus and His miracles? Because a male entity that says he researched, unknown and mystical factors of Jesus from twelve to thirty years, told me something that has not been put in the Bible. "Before Jesus was baptized, he was already producing miracles. At twenty-six years old, he demonstrated in front of numbers of people. He scooped up clay and tossed it well many times between his two hands. Then his two hands began to separate from one another and out of its hands came out a dove transformed. His hands were perfectly cleaned of all clay."

The Healers or the Doctors: The Galactic Missionaries

We as the God duo are going to work from another realm at night and on the ground daily from now on, but in invisibility. As I said previously, there is great deal of work, sacrifice, and constant focus.

My chakras that day made a sound that attracted the attention and the help of the Zeta Reticulan people, and I was told to correct my path and recenter myself. The path I walked on was pink, and I was told to adjust and walk straight back in the center of my pink path again.

I remember it was a Tuesday. I had just come back home from my yoga class, had taken a shower, changed, and headed to the office. I suddenly experienced an altered state of consciousness that occurred spontaneously. While deep in this expanded state, I had a close encounter with a monk. He was sitting inside the office waiting for me.

Within my altered state, he began to tell me the story about Christianity that was based on the teaching of the Essene. He said that it will trigger something in me and will remind me of something as doctor of light VIE and an expert and doctor of sound frequency as your blue flame.

NEW CENTURY, NEW AGE, NEW EXPERIENCES

He then went on saying that the family of Jesus interacted with extraterrestrial beings and lived with them. These celestial beings came down from another realm and communicated and lived with the Essene. Not only that, they took humans into the terrestrial realm and transformed them into angelic beings. Jesus called it the light body. Jesus was taught into it as a young man. It is an extraterrestrial teaching that was taught in the thirteen-star system.

All these star systems are connected by a system of stargate, a portal that accesses the beings and body of light. These are the Essene that have accomplished the circle and have fully manifested their light body and are now ascended to the celestial realm, the celestial city of Sion.

Two thousand years ago, a brotherhood of holy men and women, living together in a community, carried within themselves all of the seeds of Christianity and of future Western civilization. This brotherhood, more or less prosecuted, brought forth people that changed the face of the world, and through the course of history, Jesus, Mary, Saint Ann, Joseph, and John the Evangelist were among the founders of what would later be called Christianity and were Essenes.

They possessed an advanced knowledge and worked hard in secret. These Essenes were for the triumph of the light over the darkness of the humankind. They felt entrusted with a mission and were supported in this effort by highly evolved beings who directed the brotherhood, the saints, and the master of wisdom. They accorded great importance to the teaching of Moses as well as to the revelation of Enoch. They knew how to communicate with the angelic beings and had solved the question of the origin on evil on earth. One of their major preoccupations was to protect themselves from any evil spirits' contact.

The Essenes considered themselves the guardians of the divine teaching. They were the light that shines in the darkness and invites the darkness to change into light. The Essenes differentiated between the drowsy, sleeping souls and the awakened. Their task was to help, comfort, and relieve the sleeping souls, to try to awaken the drowsy souls, and to awaken souls. Only the awakened souls could be initiated into the mysteries of brothers and sisterhoods called the School of Prophets by the Hebrews and the Healers, or the Doctors, by the Egyptians.

They were students of Plato's works. Plato described the earth as a 3-D pentagram web into which the soul incarnates and must ascend from. He learned from the Egyptian that the human body is a geometrical form to interfere with the dodecahedron and its pentagon grid. Socrates told Plato that he saw the true earth from space. The dodecahedron was used as a teaching tool to instruct the initiate to know oneself as an energy system like the earth.

The empowerment teaching was given to the Essene by the heavenly ones, sons and daughters of heaven.

The Essene came to Egypt and began working with the Jewish mystics and other mystics.

After a couple of centuries, the teaching was split in two different teachings, known as the great and the small chariots or the vehicles of enlightenment and called by the Essene the Merkaba. They believe that the body becomes the chariot of the soul. One teaching followed the doctrine of the elders. They seek to become perfected saints who attain enlightenment, and this is your goal on earth.

The great vehicles develop the idea that enlightenment can be activated in one lifetime by anyone, not just the monks and nuns.

These celestial beings were living with them, teaching them and assisting humans in transforming themselves into angels.

The ancient practice of ascension, this has a great implication for Christianity.

Tibetans also teach that the human body needs to have the body accelerated so it can be spun into a vortex of energy that manifests the five colors of the body of light called the rainbow body. This is the primary celestial form of the angelic beings, and once they achieve the rainbow body, they have the ability to shift back and forth between the physical body and the immaterial celestial body.

The gnostic wisdom tradition and Essene were a group of Jewish mystics that were living in Jerusalem and Alexandria. They were known as the most elite scholars of their time and deeply interested in one singular subject: how can human beings transform into celestial beings or angels?

When we talk about ascension, the Essene tells that when you ascend, you go to Jerusalem where there is the twelve-gated city. The leftover radiation from the Big Bang makes you feel like you live in a finite universe that is shaped like a dodecahedron and reassembles to a holograph. "The universe is a hologram, and the human body is a holographic body of light and energy, and you know it, VIE," said the monk.

In AD 66, Rome had enough of this super natural things happening and the Temple of Solomon lighting up during the day stories. One million Jews were exterminated by the Roman Empire to eliminate this teaching and take back control of the Temple of Solomon.

Some monks and missionaries were sent to Alexandria to integrate with philosophers and mystics of the great city of the philosophers. These mystics established an embassy outside the wall of Alexandria and influenced a lot of the Essenes and early Christianity.

In my close encounter, the monk continued, "The Mandala on the back of the Vajra that you carry around your neck, VIE, helps everyone that glimpses or stares at it to awaken and receive the download for ascension. Your Vajra was recorded back in 326 BC where Alexander the Great invaded India."

In 1947, a fleet of UFOs in a triangle shape were flying across the sky. In July, the *Roswell Daily* reported "RAAF Captures Flying Saucer on Ranch in Roswell Region. No Details of Flying Disk Are Revealed."

In 2015, thousands of people in two separate areas saw a floating city in the skies above China. The Communist atheist soviet government, during the Cold War, promoted a military psychological operation, an ancient astronaut hypothesis, to destroy the religious faith in the Judeo-Christian roots, that we can be transformed in a split second, explaining away biblical miracles and supernatural events. The Essene talked about floating above the city of Jerusalem.

VIE

The great mystery called Raz by the Essene is a teaching that transformed them into angels and granted them access to hidden realities. That was the base of the Christianity, and in 1952, the government, which did not want the people to know about it, covered up everything with some fake stories to cover the coming of the New World Order.

The Roman Empire became the Nazis, now the Cabal, and today the UN thinks of eliminating all borders and genders to create an atheistic human race. They prefer to see you focused on flying saucers than to see humans ascend with the angels. The Roman Empire stepped in to eliminate the teaching. Joined by the Freemasons, the Jesuit and the CIA are controlled by the Vatican.

WHEN SCIENCE MADE YOU LOSE SPIRITUALITY AND HARMONY

We manifested ourselves on earth after conferring with the galactic federation that allowed us to come back and work intimately with you. We came to help you make the necessary changes to create a new world based on peace and wisdom. Our star family has been the first of your races. It is now 79,743 years that we have been visiting your planet. We came back to help you, not only to understand the world you live in, learn the lesson from it, and grow spiritually, but also win the battle against the Lucifer cult that controls earth. We are the God duo also known as CHADD and VIE.

The darkness on your planet started in 1953 to destroy the human molecule. We are here to help but not to change your evolution. However, understand that there is no ascension without spirituality.

The civilization on planet earth has changed and is moving to an age of mind and spirit. The next major event in history will be open with life forms from other worlds, and you will finally take your place in the family of life in the universe. The change has already begun, and its timing is very important since the human civilization is in the beginning of the transformation to a state of consciousness, and it will ever change the way life is on earth. You are the light.

Our star planet has thousands of years of advanced technology with understanding that are stimulating the consciousness through information. Our goal is for you to reach a new phase of evolution that focuses mainly on spirituality. We are telepaths and our technology is far more advanced than your known technology today. Because of our telepathic nature, we have no health problems and can live seven hundred years. The Indian Cherokees as well as other Indian Americans have some of our genes.

We came to show you how not to use money, politics, and religious doctrines. This has been used to keep you under control and stop your evolution.

In our own planet, goods are free and based on contribution to the society, and we pass 80 percent of our life on becoming masters of trade. We are fifth dimensional frequency; we are nonjudgmental beings of pure love.

Our weapon is simple, light and love.

You have been colonized by extraterrestrial beings from Lemuria, Atlantis, including the reptilians. You also had the integration of alien extraterrestrial beings, such as Lyra, Sirius—some descendants of the Lyrans consisting of scientists, engineers, and agriculture specialists that have explored the possibility of others visiting your planet have entered the data in their mothership.

Our technology has made possible for us to travel anywhere in the universe at a speed faster than the speed of light. We are able to use earth undersea operation, and we are very concerned about the misuse of your scientists on earth and worried that you will destroy it and yourself.

Your sciences have made you lose all spirituality and harmony. You must become responsible and create some future for the greater good of all or you will suffer from it.

We are here to educate, guide you, and tell you the truth that his hidden to you.

If our star family suddenly today would fill the skies with their spacecraft, people on earth would probably fall into some of panic and it would create confusion. Governments might fall or lose control, people would begin to think of themselves as earth citizen, and the

NEW CENTURY, NEW AGE, NEW EXPERIENCES

earth would never the same because of the knowledge of science life and philosophy, and it could have devastating effect on the religious, political, social, economic, and political structures.

Too much and too fast information would overwhelm you, though it could also be a great time to discover new things and learn from them.

As you will move into the cosmos, you will enter in contact with other races that live differently, living with different customs and mannerisms. The earth will start to go through wonderful changes when the contact with these other beings will happen.

The greater event in earth history is unfolding today.

The church is a house that is badly divided against itself that need to unite. "The Lord Thy God is One," so we are here, CHADD and VIE, to guide you into changing the way you live on earth and create peace among humans. We have a knowledge that can be used to enlighten your world that will help you resolve the differences that separate you on earth and prepare you to fit with the universal family on the otherworld. Until now, all the different races on your planet have been unsuccessful to learn to live together. You could not come to terms with the many social customs and ideologies.

Through a higher intelligence, through us, you are forced to examine yourselves, and we hope that it will help you move to a new level of awareness that can facilitate a peaceful coming together to the many nations.

Control Your Mind to Free Yourself

The Olmecs are the first Mesoamerican civilization and want to come back to advise and assist. The Olmecs were the first major civilization in Guatemala and Mexico following a progressive development in Soconusco and the modern Southwestern Pacific lowlands of Guatemala. They lived in the tropical lowlands of south-central Mexico, in the present-day states of Veracruz and are very happy as the planet is about to win and defeat the cabals through a multistage battle.

They explain that mankind's duality is represented by the two parts of the brain. In reality, the logical functioning of the brain is necessary only in the lower dimensions. What seems logical is what appears in the reality that you are seeing and that you have created. When this is fully recognized, the left brain becomes unnecessary. It is more blocking you than being a tool. When you are able to overcome your thinking that is logical, you can shape into something logical or that you can shape or be somewhere else in an instant. You will be able to fly and receive telepathically and even pass your hand through a wall. It is also your logical mind that dictates that you cannot pass your hand through a wall—with manipulation of molecular frequency, all things are possible. To access this fully, it means not trying to logically understand but knowing, feeling, and grasping concepts without words.

You are a technological society, and for the third dimensional functioning you need, or had the need for in the past, the greater functioning of logic and understanding is needed. You have been learning the basics, and now is the time to graduate. You have the ability to change from one thing to another, to change your cellular structure, your energy body.

The front of the brain above the third eye, all around the area where the pituitary gland is located, becomes connected underneath to the back of the brain. It is called the substantia nigra, an aura unknown by doctors and scientists. Within this dark aura of the brain lies the capabilities of molecular change, totally restructuring of the body. What it means is that all the things then that you cannot see with your eyes or understand with the logical mind will become apparent to you. This is when the beauty of the silence arises, simply because in the silence, the only language is the telepathic language of feeling. It is how you feel it is right-brained. The energy of telepathy knows no boundaries. Telepathy spans a universe. It can take you from one place to another in a whole essence and is present in another dimension.

This is why the archon woman working for the elite decided to block my third eye. I called my friend shaman Kat for confirmation and help. She said that every time my third eye was opening, they would make it close. What they totally forgot, or ignored, is the power of my heart that functions the same way. They could not trick me!

Parallel Universes, Parallel Dimensions, and Parallel Lifetimes Exist

Everything happens about the same time. There is no time. Time is an illusion. This planet is probably the only one place, the only species, that has found a way to measure what does not exist.

Thousands of other dimensions exist that you go in and out all the time without knowing it. The reality is not what you think. Everything is energy; everything is an illusion.

Earth is the lowest, densest, and heaviest planet in the universe to live on. It is the most difficult planet to live on at the bottom.

CHADD and VIE say that the biggest lesson you came here on the earth to learn is how to manipulate energy and create your world. You have to learn to create because your mind is powerful, very powerful. Life is a game; it's just a play. You are also the scriptwriter but your script isn't written. It is written as you go along.

Do not be trapped into thinking that there is no way out. You can create anything you want and this is the goal. This is the main thing of being alive. It's knowing and learning how to create.

We are now moving into a new earth. We are into shifting and we are bringing all these abilities back, and this is what you are supposed to learn how to do, as you cannot have your own movie by yourself. You have to have other people in. You have to have backdrop people,

NEW CENTURY, NEW AGE, NEW EXPERIENCES

even though they are not real. Your family and close friends are real; all the other ones are only energy and not real. They are only filling as background energy. They are holographic.

To create, you should meditate on what you want to create in your life. You must be clear about it and then release it. It will unfold by itself as long as you are clear on your intention.

CHADD's Mission

I heard Maximus, my passed away dog, barking behind the door, then for the second time, I was awakened by voices talking very close. What they were saying was impossible to understand first. It was not understandable enough until it became suddenly clear. They read my mind and adjusted the frequency so that it became clear enough for me to write about it.

"Ruins of an ancient civilization buried under three kilometers of ice were discovered lately while the ruins date back to the first Nazi German expedition. Archeologists have been permitted to excavate in Antarctica and other scientists. Their release will astonish the scientific communities."

Under the Ultra program, clean entities enrolled CHADD for a secret mission knowing that the system would not guess or expect that they were going to use him.

CHADD was given the mission to travel in remote viewing in Antarctica, and he saw and heard everything. A man called Jim was taken by a spacecraft of one of the seven civilizations of the underground. Jim's trip to Antarctica was to confirm what had been previously reported by different sources in the US Air Force. The

NEW CENTURY, NEW AGE, NEW EXPERIENCES

Antarctic excavations were real, and Jim was the primary witness to it with CHADD.

George is an inside secret space program person who later on had a mission to find out about multiple abductions. George shared with Jim some of his knowledge of Antarctica.

It was a civilization led by the pre-Adamite that was twelve to fourteen feet in height with elongated skulls. They also found three oval-shaped mother ships of approximately fifty kilometers in diameter. One of the three ships had been excavated and inside was a smaller spacecraft. The pre-Adamites were of extraterrestrial origin and had reached the earth about fifty-five thousand years ago. The pre-Adamite found has been frozen in a cataclysm that had occurred about twelve thousand years ago.

Most of advanced technologies and the remains of the pre-Adamites themselves have been removed from an archeological site to be made public. Also ancient artifacts from other locations will be brought from warehouses and preselected for public release. It will be accentuated on the terrestrial elements of frozen civilization not to shock the population. The archeologists have been working with the remains and were told to keep secret what they have seen.

CHADD said that he heard that it will probably be scheduled as a distraction from upcoming war crimes against global elites, as some leaks of information concerning international pedophiles circles and child trafficking. That has been found in one of the various underground work bases belonging to the interplanetary business composite, an ongoing corporate secret space program based in Antarctica.

Up to date, everything seems to have been shared either by George or some internal sources. CHADD witnessed their advanced technologies in the main underground city where he was taken. He also witnessed the encounters, many times, with a woman, Ginger of the anchart, who was Jim's guide on many trips to the inner earth in Antarctica. CHADD said there is another important figure who is a commander of the US Navy that was Jim's initial contact. The US Navy commander that is with a secret space alliance comprising of the secret space fleet program of the navy, along with others deserted from secret space programs to Antarctica and deep space. And there is also a man by the name of Alfonsi that is another important figure who joined a few years ago, Alfonsi and two representations of the inner earth civilization.

One of the two is an Asian-looking race that was met during meeting with the representatives of the seven civilizations of the inner earth. Then Jim and the others were taken by the Anshar spacecraft to an underdeveloped part of the ruins. It's an area that nearby scientific teams have not reached, so it was still untouched, and they were shown the full extent of the civilization that has been frozen. The bodies were twisted and contorted in several frozen states, as Jim commented, and a result of an obvious catastrophe by the state of the body.

The instantaneous freezing of the pre-Adamite civilizations was not only a case of this kind of catastrophe that affected an ancient civilization; the theory that poles change has been regular occurrence in earth's history.

The pre-Adamites were very thin, and by looking at their bodies, it was evident they had evolved on a planet with a lower gravitational environment. There were also many different types of normal-sized humans—some with elongated skulls and others with a short tails very similar to the pre-Adamite.

CHADD said that the pre-Adamites conducted biological experiments on the planet's indigenous humans. Alfonsi had a camera and took a lot of pictures, then sank into several of the frozen bodies an instrument and took biological samples, saying that the samples and photos would be given to the scientists from the secret space program alliance to study.

There were rolls of a metal alloy engraved with some type of their writing. The Anjar and other civilization representatives of the inner earth were collecting as many of these rolls as they could. The Anjar were adding the historical records of the frozen civilization to the library; they have an impressive library and many ancient artifacts from various civilizations.

The Anjar ships traveled through the ice to reach the ruins and could move through the walls using its advanced technologies.

NEW CENTURY, NEW AGE, NEW EXPERIENCES

The pre-Adamite discovery is expected to be made public soon, and Jim's visit and confirmation of the discovery of Antarctica seems to have big implication into it. Disclosure of the Antarctica ruins seems to be imminent as a number of variables factors impact on how much would be revealed to the world while keeping secrecy about the ongoing programs to weaponize the alien artifacts has been given to Jim. The goal is to eventually release some information to begin with, but not on the technologies, especially those that are clearly extraterrestrial.

Many high dignitaries including the Vatican and the Orthodox Pope and members of the government, when they visited Antarctica, provided circumstantial evidence that an important discovery has been made in the Antarctic. Antarctica is basically controlled by the reptilian. Thanks to the remote viewing, we now have evidence of the extent of the Antarctica discovery, and ongoing scientific excavation are expected to announce some elements of the discovery soon.

It is a multidimensional effort to excavate specific, important regions of Antarctica in search of a frozen alien civilization created by refugees as the stabilizing of the continent's massive ice shelf, the secret military bases in Antarctica, or the using of some artifacts for weapons development. This is a violation of the 1959 Antarctica Treaty in which it clearly stipulates that the continent's resources will be only used for scientific purposes.

CHADD said that the pre-Adamite arrived fifty-five years ago and established output devices all over Antarctica. They created the hybrid species *Homo capensis*, which became the ruling elites or demigods in ancient South American, Asian, and European societies. The pre-Adamites established their main base right over ancient builder race technology. It is a race who established a travel grid throughout the galaxy using traversable wormholes hundreds of millions years ago. When they first arrived in Antarctica, they quickly took control through their advance technologies over the area populated by human settlement at this time. With their advanced medical technologies, they then began many experiments and created hybrids (the archons) that became the servant class.

CHADD reported that the pre-Adamite programs interrupted twenty-two genetic experiments ran by human-looking extraterrestrials first established five hundred thousand years ago. A super federation comprising forty to sixty of these races established competing genetic engineering programs with surface humanity. The pre-Adamites are also engaged in conflict with the human-looking ETs running their twenty-two genetic experiments as well as the reptilians doing likewise for global influence, given that the pre-Adamites established a physical presence on earth that give them an advantage in establishing ruling bloodlines over the Americas, Asia, and Europe.

The humans who escaped into the earth interior to avoid multiple surface catastrophes monitored how the different extraterrestrial races competed against each other's influence and power over surface humanity, who is still recovering from global catastrophes. One of the inner earth races that pride themselves on their pure human bloodlines, the Anshar, had a historical connection to the human settlement in Antarctica. However, the Anshar did not cooperate with the pre-Adamites because they considered them to be sociopaths in term of their treatment to the native Antarctica population and other regions of surface humanity where they had established colonies. The pre-Adamites used to treated human in antiquity in a similar manner to how modern humans treat dogs in term of crossbreeding for multiple purposes. The pre-Adamites along with the reptilians are a big problem for all humanity

"They created hybrid species because *Homo sapiens* are in control of the monetary system hiding in the Vatican. They are the greys and psychopathic bankers responsible for the depopulation on earth and reducing it to slavery. They are the Jesuit, illuminati, draco-reptilian, gray occupiers, manipulator Anunnaki ETs, and others. These cornhead hominids appeared during the Egyptian Pharaoh Akhenaton's and his wife Nefertiti's time. These *Homo sapiens* are the earth's high cabal and covert controller," (Dr. Edward Spencer).

The reptilians, the Nordics, the Avenge, and the Anshar were interacting with the ancient Sumerians to a system in the recovery of their civilization after the great catastrophe that destroyed Atlantis.

NEW CENTURY, NEW AGE, NEW EXPERIENCES

The Anunnaki were indeed the reptilians, but the other groups that interacted with them also were referred to by the same name. A small number of the pre-Adamites survived the catastrophic freezing in the Antarctic regions by going inside stat chambers in the largest of their three mother ships.

Many excavations are occurring in multiple places in Antarctica by various nations to obtain the most advanced technologies. Some are in direct competition. All the nations involved there in the Antarctic excavations are capable of a disclosure release on their own, but they are all working together and in negotiations to do it in a coordinated manner. CHADD thinks that the disclosure will begin at the same time with the prosecutions of the elites involved in human trafficking and pedophilia and other crimes, which includes the blackmailing of the political leaders, academic industrialists, and military officials.

The recent presidential administration action to dismiss forty-six district attorneys was because of their inaction in moving forward with these prosecutions. The concern is that the Chinese, Russians, or even smaller nations could start announcements on Antarctica if the negotiations do not start and the US fails to move ahead. The global cabal has grown with the economic power mounting in ASRA (American Society of Anesthesia and Pain Medicine) Europe and North America and continues to gradually diminish.

A battle that took place over the Antarctica skies early last year began when teardrop-shaped ships came out of the sea in the Ross Ice Shelf and thought they would escape into deep space. These ships flew out of bases belonging to a corporate-run space program called the Interplanetary Corporate Conglomerate's (ICC/Nazis) battle over Antarctica. The ships belonged to the Cabal, who were allied to another program called the Dark Fleet. They were filled with global elites trying to escape an anticipated global chaos that could be caused by an upcoming solar event.

Dozens of delta-shaped crafts appeared then as the Dark Fleet of the Cabal vessels (working for the Draco) reached the upper atmosphere. Their teardrop ships were badly injured in the battle by the delta-shaped crafts in the battle and had to come back to their base. The attacking delta crafts were built using earth technologies of this conglomerate that only came from Russia and Asian syndicates belonging to an earth alliance. They revealed that the earth had success in bridging the technological gap with the most advanced space technologies known to exist.

There is an exodus of elite groups to South America and Antarctica, groups of high level syndicates that were seen moving huge amounts of personal items and supplies to the underground of South America, mostly Brazil. But they could not leave the earth and so chose to flee instead to South America. These people were transported to Antarctica via black submarines the size of container ships through one of the doorways used by the elites into the vast water-filled tunnel systems throughout South America and Antarctica that extended all the way from Mexico through South America down into Antarctica.

Bariloche in Argentina is where Adolph Hitler took refuge after World War II, and it became the unofficial headquarters of the Fourth Reich.

There are two excavations conducted at the same time by other nations across Antarctica, which again are affecting the entire Antarctica shelf. It is destabilizing the Ross Ice Shelf and other ice shelves. One process to destabilize the Ross Ice Shelf is the use of large pressurized steam holes to reach the pre-Adamite ruins. They are connected to large pressurized tanks in which large bags of water are hit with microwave beams to cause them to explode with steam opening into a large area. Another process uses natural phenomenon that involves harnessing powerful geothermal vents caused by volcanic activity deep below Antarctica.

During his remote trip underground, CHADD was shown some radio-type gadgets. One of these gadget could reportedly tune in on conversations taking place in various part of the globe including in the offices of the Bank of England. The Bank of England was one of the earliest institutions founded on the expendable paper money system. That system was largely the creation of mystics and revolutionaries affiliated with the brotherhood network and have continued to be a principal center of that system up until today.

THE ZETA RETICULANS

We are living a new era, and if human beings want to ascend, they better hurry to be more preoccupied by researching and understanding the truth hidden to them by the cabal, the elite in power. Thousands of children are disappearing every year, many human beings are missing, and children are forced to receive vaccinations that are slowing down their defenses and getting them sick, when they do not die from it, and no one is reacting. Though people are getting into the street to manifest against the new government, they are manipulated by the elites, but not enough parents appear to defend their own children. Isn't it sad? They are unfortunately awakened.

The Zeta Reticuli binary star system lives about thirty-nine years from earth. A long time ago, the Zetans had to battle the reptilians also, but they have evolved now.

My chakras made a frequency that attracted the attention of *Asuba* and the Zetan beings to help me. The female archon, a reptilian hybrid servant of the cabal, in her despair to stop me, implanted some alien parasites in my body and my frequency changed. The Zetan people read my chakras and came to my assistance.

The Zetans are looking like the gray alien, but these two races have a completely different agenda. Both of these races live in the Reticuli binary star system. Their physical difference is that the gray does not reassemble humans as much as the Zetas do, and the gray's agenda is very unfriendly toward humans.

The Zeta Reticulans have a big difference to the human appearances unlike the gray. They have eyes that are all black with no pupils or iris. They have large heads with no hair and small hard ears-like bumps on the sides of their heads, long fingers, and some are webbed. They have small seemingly human noses as well as human-looking chins and facial expressions. They are about three feet in height. The Zeta Reticulans wear silver jumpsuits that cover their entire bodies including half of the neck, the upper torso, and legs but not the head or hands.

They are highly technological and scientifically advanced and ahead of humans in their development by a few million years. They lived in the Zeta system but have become space travelers, and many spend their entire existence in space. They possess the knowledge of time travel and can shift from the third to the fourth dimension and can help others shift through these dimensions as well by shifting their frequency, and Asuba has decided to raise my frequency level since our second contact. The variety of Zeta appearances is because of their extensive travel and settlement in different environment and their adaptation to space and travel.

Various grays have different histories, and some are known to have overemphasized their focus on technology to the detriment of other qualities. They have now evolved to be able to integrate with their technology in a symbiotic relationship and have learned to balance their spirituality with their technological dependency. They are scientific problem-solvers and use energy transformers.

Zetas can integrate with the consciousness of anything, and it is how they can create. They understand that their tools have also consciousness, and they work with that consciousness. Their ships' equipment responds to their telepathic communication and are considered live beings with dense consciousness, which can be reached and they connect to it and control it.

NEW CENTURY, NEW AGE, NEW EXPERIENCES

Zetas have been involved with the evolution of many third dimensional species including humans because of their advances in genetic engineering and their ability to still work within a third dimensional environment. The Zeta Reticulans possess extremely advanced mental-like, telepathic, telekinetic, and other high mental functions.

They appear emotionless but are expert at reading frequency and do not need physical expression to show their feelings. They operate from heightened emotional states and are not influenced by denser emotions and are often called upon for upgrading species from the third to the fourth dimension.

Zetas can manipulate energy fields, which allow them to heal and create projections and alter sensations. They do it with genetic methods to which there is an energetic component and through teaching the spiritual principles to help species learn to use their psychic acumen. They are evolutionary helpers that watch over species progression.

Vedas also assist with modulating star seed energies to integrate with third-dimensional physical bodies for incarnation. Vedas live for their sense of interconnectedness and without it feel lost. They also need the understanding that comes with connecting to each other and with all other beings as well. This is why they form collectives that work together to solve many problems. Their focus is advancement and species evolution and how the soul can evolve by means of experiencing different forms.

The Zetas have been involved by means of experiencing different forms. The Zetas have been with earth periodically since the first life-forms were established here and with humanity since their earliest evolutionary leaps. They have always been here as helpers in human development and assisting with DNA upgrades.

They have been asked by the galactic councils to create an earth human-Zeta hybrid in order to help humans gain a new level of consciousness and further the ongoing universal expression.

I remember my encounters with three of them. I was impressed by the black eyes, for me similar to the horse's eyes. The first time was in one of the conventions in Florida. I was busy preparing to do a few light reconnections in demonstration to the public. When I turned to face the public, I found myself face-to-face, eye to eye with two women. One was an angel with striking eyes, and the other one had the specific Zetan eyes—all black, no iris. I was taken by surprise and wondered what they wanted from me.

The angel answered my question even before I asked and said that she was the one that brought the other woman as she wanted confirmation. Confirmation of what, I did not even ask. All I know is that my vibratory transformation energy was so strong that the hybrid alien told me that she could not walk and had to wait and rest a few minutes.

The second time was also in a convention doing the same thing. It began that time by three persons from the elite approaching me—two women and one man. The man was the only one to talk. I still remember this self-sufficient look, pointing toward my light with his finger and asking me, "What's that?" One of the women had a badge on which you could read "Psychic." The man asked me then his second and last question, still with a condescending look on his face. "Are organs energy?"

When I answered his question, the man became pale, and he and the psychic woman left as fast as they could, without a word. I saw them taking the door and rapidly leaving the convention. The other woman had obviously been sent to experience my work without being aware of it and the psychic woman to observe and report the effect on her. She took her place and sat while the Zetan man sat on the right side floor not far from me and paid close attention to what I was doing.

When all was finished, the woman got off the chair and asked, "What am I doing here?" She shook her head and left.

The following day is where I met the third alien. I went to the organic grocery store, and here was another one following me all around inside the store. When he realized that I was mentioning him to my friend, he left. I never saw any since. Then years later, the Zetans reappeared in my life to help me from their invisible world.

The Zetas have obtained a reputation for their much misunderstood abductions and human experiments. It has been suspected by many that they do these abductions to obtain DNA from human beings in order to prolong their own species, but nothing could be further from the truth. They already have the skill to clone their bodies, which are well adapted for space travel and shift their souls into new bodies. The truth is that the abductions made to obtain human DNA are made by the gray aliens and not the Zetas.

The Zeta Reticulans do not feel fear the way humans do and thus appear cold to this emotion. It is seen by many beings that fear is a detriment to human evolution and galactic relations. This is one of the attributes the Zetas attempted to diminish in the new hybrids. It is true that these hybrids will not exist on earth alone and that Zeta beings will in some cases transfer their consciousness into these hybrids. They are meant to be an evolutionary leap of potential expression for many in the universe to experience.

Sassani means "beams of light." The Sassani race are also known as the Shakani. They are a humanoid hybrid extraterrestrial alien race living on earth. The Sassani are genetic hybrids between Earth humans and Zeta Reticulans that live on the planet Dasani. They possess a combination of the best characteristics of both races. They have the Zeta telepathic abilities, longevity sensibility, scientific and intellectual capacities as well as humanity's vital emotional, sexual, and physical aspects, and the very human curiosity, the predilection for speedy advancement.

THE SIRIANS AND THE ANDROMEDANS

They came to help against elite families that control the Vatican and the corporation (the incorporation of the Apostle Peter). The Cabal controls the world and the CIA, and they do not want you to ascend.

The Roman Catholic Church has a long history of tyranny and oppression driven by the desire to control through their inquisitions. The "Unam sanctam" is the first express trust created by the Catholic Church, and it says that all of the souls in the world belong to the Roman Catholic Church and they do because no one has challenged their claim. Your birth certificate is the title of the soul that they own in their registries. They have registered you and that is the title to your soul.

The Inquisition began because many people were waking up to the tyranny and oppression of the Roman Catholic Church in the early 1300s. The RCC killed these people because of their need to control humanity. Two hundred years later during the Renaissance, the *Hermetica* was written, from which the Bible draws its inspiration. This knowledge was also suppressed by the RCC.

In AD 325, the emperor Constantine the Great made a donation to Pope Sylvester, saying, "Saint Peter is the Apostle of Jesus of whom Jesus gave this kingdom of Earth to; therefore, we are going to claim taxes."

The Lion People (Sirius A)

The planet Sirius is the brightest star in the heavens, a binary star composed of Sirius A and around it moving Sirius B. Different races inhabit this system, and these races have a long history with the earth. They have had benevolent dealings with Lemuria, Atlantis, and Egypt more recently. One of these races on Sirius A is a humanoid species known as the lion people.

These are high-frequency benevolent beings, highly intelligent and creative, and perhaps the best depiction of these people can be found in the Egyptian image of the goddess Sekhmet—part humanoid, part lion. This race of beings is much taller than humans at this time of evolution. Many star seeds on earth have a strong karmic connection to this race of beings. These beings are connected to the blue lodge, which acted as guardians or benefactors of this planet for many thousands of years before Atlantis. The lion people have contributed to this great genetic experiment that is humanity in a positive way. They are among other things geneticists and have helped develop life forms of various kinds for planets and stars in the universe. They are great explorers and have interceded in crucial times in our long history, in times of crisis.

VIE

Sirian alien races are very different. Some extraterrestrials from the Sirius star system are benevolent and good, which is mostly around Sirius A, and around Sirius B, they are mostly evil. There are many humanoid and humanoid species. Some are aquatic; others are reptilian. The famous aquatic extraterrestrial race is the Nomonos people, who visited earth many years ago and contacted the dragon tribe from Africa in Mali. They gave the Malistes incredible astronomic knowledge, which exceeded the scientists' knowledge at that time. There are many Sirians helping earth to ascend alongside the Pleiadians and Andromedans.

ANDROMEDANS

They are among the most evolved civilizations working with the earth at time of ascension. They live in the constellation of Andromeda and exist from 3-D up to 12-D. It is a spiral galaxy of 2.5 million light-years away from earth. Their technology is far beyond anything experienced on the earth, as is their connection with the Creator. They are always present when your soul expands, becoming a more truthful expression of the Creator. They are overseeing and supporting humans' ascension as are many light beings. They support the humans in moving in harmony as one with the ascension energies and waves anchoring on the inner planes.

The Arcturians

The Arcturians are an advanced, positively oriented alien race helping the planet to ascend. The Arcturians travel the universe in advanced spaceships. They have one particular ship for healing transmissions. The light ship Athena, which is part of an armada of ships, keeps a friendly eye on earth at this time of ascension.

It's a huge ship that was orbiting somewhere between the asteroid belt and Jupiter at the time of their transmission when I entered in contact with them for a healing session. Athena is an equipped ship with light technology that holds many specialized healers, including the Arcturian medical assistance team for this transmission. The Arcturians were particularly helpful at this time in assisting humanity clearing out any negative alien races. Their agendas are based on manipulation. They are very good at cleaning out any energetic cord implants, karmic connections with lower races.

I was guided that afternoon to listen to their healing transmission.

The Arcturians asked me to get comfortable and be ready for their medical assistance team. They helped me shed layers of density, repaired my etheric body, and made repairs at the cellular level of my physical body. When needed, they can help to upgrade the nervous system to accommodate more light and activate layers of the light body.

NEW CENTURY, NEW AGE, NEW EXPERIENCES

They guided me to the time of the full treatment, asking me to remain conscious and also took care of adjusting my Vajra. My feet became really cold at some point, and I took one minute up to cover myself, and they reminded me to surrender and trust the process, to stay conscious while they were working on regulating my chakras and raising my energy level to the right level.

It was quite interesting to hear them use the light and the sound. They adjusted my right inner ear chakra, and I was happy when it popped up open.

I finally grew so relaxed and sleepy at the end that I felt asleep and left my body.

AYLA, A WHISTLE-BLOWER: SOMETHING IS GOING WRONG

Ayla became an important whistle-blower when a serious car accident left her near death. While she was in a coma, an angel appeared and told her that she would be of great service to humanity. She would be handicapped though, as her body has been severely damaged in the accident, but her mission now was to use the large stored knowledge from her CIA position she had before the accident.

She asked me to move the car a little bit forward so she could get in the back seat. She sat at the edge of the seat, then slid herself in, her legs resting now on the seat.

"It was not easy to find you," she said. "Drive me to the location I will indicate to you. It's one of the last few ones not under camera. We need privacy for what I have to tell you."

Once arrived, Ayla began to tell me a little bit about what happened to her and why she contacted me.

"My angel gave me your name while I was in a coma. I have information to share with you. After that you have witnessed the mind control, now I am here to tell you about the environment that is collapsing and the economy on the edge of collapse. We are at a time for courage and a time for truth. Autism is an epidemic, exponential academic, and humans must stop accepting intimidation. The tyrannical government overreaches our entire lives. They have been scarring, intimidating for way too long, and it is time to bring back the Constitution, 'We the people.'

Before my accident, I worked for the CIA and I had access to much information, but they made me sign a nondisclosure agreement. Like everyone that gets a job and obtain knowledge of these covert programs sign an agreement, the AF geoengineering program has to sign the agreement that says, 'If you disclose anything that you know about this program, you can be terminated or we can force criminal penalties and you can be put in prison.' That is how they stop employees and all people to talk. They do not want to go to jail, lose their jobs, and have their lives destroyed.

There are chemtrails all over the country sky. Every time chemicals are sprayed over the populated areas, they fall into the purview of US code, the statutes regarding chemical and biological warfare. There are sections in a specific chapter where it talks about exceptions to this prohibition of spraying over the populated areas. There is to be a presidential directive in writing, there is a notice that has to be given to the Secretary of Health and Human Services. Written notice has to be given to each governor in each state where the spray is anticipated to occur.

Nano particles in jet fuel was a NASA program entitled "Nanotechnology and Gelled Cryogenic Fuels" with the idea that beings have oxide-coated aluminum. There is a correlation between HAARP and the enhancement that HAARP does to engineering.

A HAARP facility is an ionosphere heater, and there are about two and a half dozen of these large ground-based facilities around the globe and an unknown number of smaller RF transmitters. They appear everywhere on the radar, and in this, the radio frequencies are a huge part of the climate modification and everybody is a walking antenna.

There are many aspects other than visible trails. None of them are benevolent and none of them are in the human's best interests.

There is respiratory distress caused by chemtrails. Chemtrails are nanoparticles that are put into the air to shield the ground from the sun and block and reflect the sunlight. They are bombarded with microwave radiation from the ground that match the frequency of these particles in just the right way, and these particles then begin to heat up in the air. Then that heat is transferred to the surrounding air mass.

You have countless trillions of these particles suspended in the air that are all painted with this signal, and they all heat up at the same time and carry that air mass and all the moisture that is in it to a higher altitude where it will condense and become a powerful low-pressure system.

When you heat up the air mass, it rises and expands, and so by controlling where and when these events occur, you can control the flow of the jet stream. And this is happening in the planet at the same time. The toxics greatly affect these materials. You can line fifty of these particles up next to a single red blood cell and that is how tiny they are. They can be absorbed through the skin, and there is almost no filtration system that can be worn to prevent these things from being introduced into your body during respiration.

It is a serious matter not just at the toxic level but as an epidemiological situation in terms of infection. You can imagine what could happen if the wrong material gets sprayed in the air.

A little while ago, the New York underground subway had some alterations done, the authorities said, for "insuring air ventilation" to people in case of any underground problem.

Aluminum has a toxic effect on the white blood cells part of your immune system that exists right in your lungs, in the alveoli that is your first line of defense against infection. By suppressing the immune system in the lungs, anything else put into the air will go right into your system without your body being able to defend against it.

There is a rainbow scan or spectrometer that produces spikes wherever there is a particular color that is produced by each of the unique elements that are in it. It is used to test the air.

There is no filter to clean up the air known at that day, and chemicals show up in the water through rain samples and we cannot filter it out of water.

NEW CENTURY, NEW AGE, NEW EXPERIENCES

I am telling you, VIE, it is very important to bring this information to the public and create a daily awareness of detoxing the body and remove it. A biological effect to this is that the more aluminum is in the body, the more sensitive people are to those fields. More and more people are being energetically sensitive."

It has happened because people have been so busy with their lives trying to survive that they have gone away with it and so far. This is a wakeup call and an alert. It's almost too late to stop what is now a postconstitutional government. The people are no longer relying on the country. Sadly, the tyrannical government rules the people by subversion, force, and fear.

Exposure to toxins causes bleeding gums, bruising all over the body, short-term memory loss, severe headaches, and more. Toxins are being denied by the NSA, CIA, DIA, especially by the covert agencies engaged in nefarious operational programs, because there is a culture of fear. Everybody inside is afraid of saying anything because they know about the system about to destroy them and you, your family, and your finances. Some are driven to suicide.

There is a way to test if your body is poisoned through a hair analysis. Whatever is in your bloodstream will show up in your hair. The thing is that your body will not allow it to stay in the bloodstream, but it will show up in your hair.

Trying to get rid of it through DMPS chelation may store it in your kidneys and in your liver. Chelation procedures sometimes are toxic. Light therapy will replace the chelation.

Our body has been given abilities to remove these toxins. Magnesium is an element. Two elements of magnesium will remove one aluminum, so this must be increased.

As the body discharges the toxins, and particularly aluminum, heavy metals, mercury, etc., it goes in your colon. The three-fourth of your colon's job is to reabsorb. What happens is that the body has tremendous ability to recycle, and you have to block the recycling mechanisms on metal. Karela and other algae will do it.

It is going to take pressure of the public to denounce it. There is no defense against these chemicals that you inhale, and they go straight into your brain, and as you breathe them again, they go into your lungs and there is no defense.

Where are the whistle-blowers? Why don't they come out and blow the whistle if it is so dangerous?

The NSA spying program stores the information in the Utah Data Center in case they will need to use it against you. They have your emails, texts, cell phone conversations, all well stored in their databases. All on you, not on the terrorists. There is a massive, complex, secret mechanism in the US government. The intelligence community is so powerful that not even the Congress or the Senate can control. They shut down NSA's surveillance program. There are ten thousand secret locations inside the country, not overseas.

It all began with the king of England who had absolute power to shut down any case he deemed unacceptable, including from Congress and Senate. It has grown far worse from there. Now these procedures have been perfected. It is a science to destroy a whistle-blower. First, promotions are denied with embarrassing assignments, like a top performer is put in a corner of a building so that everyone knows. In case the whistle-blower continues, they will raise its interest rates on the credit union loans so that it's now not affordable. Their retirement funds are blocked, and they will destroy the family finances, though it's a felony for a federal agency to deny the retirement funds of an employee.

That's not all. They will refer you to the office of medical services to undergo some psychological counseling to help you sleep better at night and make you less anxious. Then when the interview is over, the document is falsified. The employee is paranoid, obsessive-compulsive, and it goes in the file, so if it ever gets to Congress or Senate or court, they will say that it went under evaluation and the person is basically unstable. They will then shut down the case as part of an intentional process.

If you report it to a newspaper that they control, the newspaper will call right away and tell this person just reported so and so.

The entire world goes wrong. Look at the European Union: it is a centralized dictatorship, a centralized one world government now, a world government that has the power to dictate to the entire

NEW CENTURY, NEW AGE, NEW EXPERIENCES

population. It is a central global dictatorship that wants one world central bank, one world currency, one world government, and one world army. They want a world army to impose the will of the one world government to any country that will resist and will not accept the European army.

The worst is that most of the politicians are not even aware of it. They do not see the reality. They need to raise their consciousness. Time has changed.

People are less and less informed. As one of my colleagues said, the country is at stake, your freedom is at stake, and this is the final hour. We sent a call for some to come out and stand with these people and have the guts and the courage to support the constitution as there is maybe half a decade at the most.

Then came out the Pizzagate, WikiLeaks, etc. Now the FBI insiders are ready to file actual criminal charges against some of the highest level of the cabal people in the government for pedophilia and all their satanic behavior. A secret grand jury has been appointed.

Once the information was shared, Ayla asked me to drop her to a bus station, and I never heard from her again.

Pyramids, Human Vibratory States, and Nine

The pyramids are the primary custodians of local density of cosmic vibrations. It generates subtle energies that have the same spiral multiple dimensions and influence all alive organisms in nature.

"All perceptible matter comes from a primary substance, filling all space, the Akasha or luminous ether, which is acted upon by life-giving prana or creative forces, calling into existence in never ending cycles all things and phenomena."

The musical frequencies modify the human vibratory states. Each object and each form emits vibration. Energies that disagree with nature and natural resonance can generate negative effects on human behavior and consciousness.

At the ascension, the rainbow colors will appear in the sky and rain will stop; it's the solar flash prophecy. The sun will come down toward the earth, and the just will be transformed (ascension) and the wicked will be consumed by it. The dark spirits plan to be gone before it happens.

The Magic of 432 Hz

I was walking toward a bungalow that overlooked the ocean. I flashed into a scene, to the light that is cosmic love. I was the light and this light had the knowledge and revealed to me that the sum frequencies of nine unify the properties of light, time and space matter, gravity, and magnetism with biology DNA code and consciousness. The whole life of a man is an electric current and his soul is the light. A light is a cosmic love by vibrating on the sound frequency 432 Hz, which equals nine. Thinking on the number 9 wall reveals the greatest truth of all, and it is an encoder of the universe. The earth vibration declared us love and tells us that she is alive.

"To create and to annihilate material substances causing them to aggregate in forms according to his desire, would be the supreme manifestation of the power of man's mind, his most complete triumph over the physical word."—Nikola Tesla

Different sounds exist at different frequencies or vibrations, and all things living are vibrational and dimensional. Vibrational frequency is the key to understanding the universe. Our brain has the ability to interpret these frequencies into what we perceive to be our physical reality. Trees, chairs, tables, persons are just energy.

VIE

All things living are vibrational, eight-dimensional. Everything you see, touch, hear, smell, or taste is made up of different wavelengths vibrating at different frequencies. There are nonphysical energies also, like our thoughts, which are different vibrations.

When your thought is positive, it is vibrating at a higher frequency; if your thought makes you feel bad, if it's a negative thought, it is vibrating at a lower frequency. For example, when you grieve or you are sad, you are in a lower frequency. If you think "I hate you," that's a lower vibration. Now if you think "I love you," that is a higher vibration. Focusing on a positive or negative thought will attract you to the same vibration and will join you together.

I Began to Stare

Like all dreams, it happened in real physical plane time. It presented itself in my waking awareness in visual form accompanied by the sounds. The information I received was vibratory, telling me what has taken place and was unfolding.

I can't see where I am driving. I am driving in fog, but it is a glowing white fog and I am inside this white light in which I am totally protected. The few people of the counsel had to bring rewards through a young man. The man in the chair is the father. He has a lot of affection on his face. It is a sweet, loving expression on his face. He knew my gift, and he has decided that now it was time for me to know that he knew. Time to be recognized by others that my work will now help us get the financial success that is coming. Only his smile fulfills you when you see it. It fulfilled me. It is great peace and a feeling of great protection also that gives total balance and harmony with a sense of great comfort. The father's face vibrates love, affection, forgiveness, knowingness—everything at the same time. Though I do not see his face, I see it—the miracle of his vision.

VIE

I stare into the white and glowing fog. I rapidly understood that the white fog is a giant cloud with the father's light in it, and I am in it. Then I am now feeling more than seeing three or four persons at maximum.

The people are preparing themselves for the audition of a singer. There is also one young man and another person and me. They want me to be a participant. They are interested with the young talented man. Now here are the details.

I am driving my car in the bright fog with no visibility in a cloudy mountain. I can't see at all where I am going. I am suddenly aware. I perceive that I am driving the top of a mountain road. I do not know if I am not driving toward a cliff, or if I am still on the road. But it does not worry me. This awareness goes away. I feel relaxed. Now I am back to see that its windy, a gentle breeze, and there is a very thin rain that adds to the fog. It is a brilliant white foggy cloud but very gentle.

The vision changes. I am singing and I continue to drive. My driving is the singing. I sing and this is all there is, and it seems to be so perfect to sing and it is so fulfilling me. I forget everything I just sing and be. It is harmony and peace and a sense of wholeness.

The song is finished and the vision changes. I see a man in a chair appearing in my vision, but I can't see who he is, though I see him clearly. It is weird but it seems OK and normal. He has a loving and affectionate expression on his face looking at me. If he was telling me that he knew, he has always known. It was evidence and I did not know. Then he looks at the other people there for the audition. He breaks the silence and finally says looking at me, "Now we are going to be able to take some vacations. VIE is making it so we can afford it. That's my VIE!"

They all looked at me now with astonishment and great respect. Someone offered me some water. I am so surprised. I can't believe what's happening. I still do not understand what has happened. Why me, I am thinking. It was supposed to be about the young man, and they are choosing to honor me. Well, it seems obvious that the young man was used as an excuse make my work known!

The Takeover

I received an interesting and weird, at the same time, phone call from someone that pretended to have done his genealogy tree and went into some weird explanation telling me that we were from the same family in the past and said that he was the Holy Grail. But he mentioned the Anunnaki and Napoleon Bonaparte while I was instead at this time focusing on the return of the Guardians that had been corrupted. He was bringing to me the biggest secret in the history of the country, he said.

Understand that there is actually eight trillion dollars unaccounted for, misappropriated, used without the knowledge of Congress or the president of the United States. The secrecy is maintained by the hybrid archons and servants of corporate and government program, in which military bases and facilities are involved. We are talking about a black budget and a criminal activity that is funding these operations through financial connections. That was initiated during 1953 to 1954.

There are two governments: the official one and the top secret special intelligence compartment that has developed around the secrecy of the UFOs.

In 1956, the Rockefeller Commission reorganized the Pentagon and the Department of Defense, CIA, and the all secret entities. It was done deliberately in such a way that it became almost impossible to penetrate by anyone. Therefore, it made it virtually impossible for any ordinary congressman or the president to access it. A system that guarantees their ignorance except that they want to release just enough information to control what is going on. The first CIA director even said that it was actually a threat to the country of the United States. Because he found out he was put aside by the neofascists who had taken over the intelligence community, the zero space community, and the large corporations. It was a deliberate takeover by the corporate states. The corporations working with the unacknowledged special access projects are not funded officially. The security programs, the president of the United States, members of Congress, the CIA directors, the secretaries of states could not access it. It was gradually happening, and by 1961 it was done.

No president since Eisenhower had the information near the level on this that would be required for the chief executive. Most CIA directors haven't either.

Science and technology, besides the antigravity, is the energy source. Gravity control is the ability to put an electromagnetic field at certain voltages and with certain angular momentum. The object becomes massless, weightless, and when mass become zero, velocity can go to infinity and then you go trans-dimensional. Using crystalline structures and very high voltages going into an object to the next object would begin to levitate. It can also be nano-crystalline materials such as metallic, almost metals, rocks, crystal, water that is crystalline, like the human body. It is the amazing electromagnetic flux field. It is the infinite field of energy that is at the root of space-time. So this was what began to develop in the '20s, taken into Army Air Force projects in the '30s and '40s and was Adolf Hitler's secret weapon.

Bringing it out would immediately make oil, gas, coal, Mobil, Exxon, cars, internal combustion engines, jet engines, ocean lines, everything that we use obsolete rapidly. Then you add to this the material and the electronics retrieved from interstellar spaceships that were shut down, plus the Nikola Tesla files integrated circuit, filter optics, and the large numbers of things that came from studying the material of these crushed ET interstellar objects. The most secret and most well-funded project into the history of the United States that nobody knew about. Imagine the eight trillion dollars in mineral assets and infrastructure would be down. But it would be a whole new world.

So the genius people put their attention to gravity control and to find out how these visitors were getting on the planet. This is very important for the national security and the secrecy.

The Office of Special Services became CIA after the World War II. CIA had the Operation Paperclip. They would put a paperclip on the file they did not want to go to Nuremburg and be executed of the people whose knowledge was so great that the government wanted them to be part of their program. They wanted what they knew. They became the foundation brought in by CIA, what became the CIA of the US space program in the 1940s and '50s.

Also since 1954, Lockheed Martin has made man-made UFOs. In the new facility, they work not just on the propulsion systems but also on the electronic warfare systems and the bio-nanotechnology.

The things that the UFO retail world of books and movies and conferences called aliens, are 100 percent man-made. They have some integrated circuits in their brains and walk around as little gray or reptilian-looking things.

But there are consequences to this kind of secrecy. It is really about blowing back to us, physically, environmentally, politically, and militarily. It is very dangerous to part the development of normal technologies to be used for powerful purposes. To keep this secret, the wet works kill people for secrecy.

Psychology board and psychological warfare—The problems connected to UFOs appear to have implications for psychological warfare as well as for intelligence and operations. They wanted to be able to set up a deception around the subject and to put out false information and use it as a cover story for classified aerospace research, so often there will be something that happens and it will look like a UFO while it would be some aerospace entity a hundred percent man-made.

Walt Disney was an asset of the CIA, and they engaged Disney Studios to make flying saucers and little green men to ridicule the subject about UFO and aliens. And now reporters and media people and CIA members as well as Congress know it's real and don't want to be ridiculed. They don't want to be laughed at.

Star Wars was also a cover story for targeting in space for interstellar spaceships using scalar weapons and not lasers.

The foo fighters were objects that flew around US aircrafts during World War II. They were sometimes just energy, and it could come down in the center of an aircraft and get out at the other end. It's a trans-dimensional nature of extraterrestrial technologies. This became a huge concern for the allies. They would disrupt electromagnetic signals and have effects in the gravity around an aircraft and on other things as the guidance system compasses. They were interplanetary spaceships, interstellar, that became very concerned about what humans were doing on earth and the risk of destroying the planet. At that time, there was a reasonable level of constitutional oversight by key members of Congressional senior people in the administration. The president then assembled a group of people who worked on the Manhattan Project and others to look at the problem. Everything has changed since 1956 since there has always been competition between PBI, CIA, and Air Force Intelligence, and it also happened between allies and alliances.

NATO, the CIA, FBI, and the European Parliament had no idea of the transnational entity unacknowledged. But when you have the president and senior members of the military left out of it and eight trillion dollars vanishing now per year and unaccounted, the country has no government. From 1950, the deep national security state until today has devolved into this unacknowledged transnational security state with representation in the UK, Canada, Australia, Brazil, China, and Russia that work on this altogether.

Running unconstitutional countries engaging in assassinations is wrong, keeping from the planet technologies that would save the earth from environment destructions and eliminate poverty within a generation. They use this technology to provoke an interstellar conflict and World War II, being totally off the reservation without any controls from the legitimate governments of the world because they knew they would not have gone with their agenda.

This is all run by a hybrid entity (archon). They are part of the government-acknowledged special access project compartmented deep-black transnational security state. These people do not seek or want peace on the planet; they love wars because there is too much money to lose.

President Kennedy had a great interest in it and was briefed on the subject, but unfortunately the matter was out of his hand and he was later killed. President Carter ran on ending this disclosure. Not only he did not get access but he was responsible for the Watergate scandal and was only a one-term president.

This is how almost a century of evolution was lost by the human race.

Once again the dark forces were trying to see to what extent I knew about them, but I just listened to what this man was telling me. He sent me an invitation to meet them, and I replied that we will see how and when we will be guided to meet and hung up.

Freemasonry, Ancient Egypt, the Islamic Destiny, and the Cabal

On that evening, my goal was to journey about anything else than to obtain accurate information about current issues in the world. But that was not what happened.

I began by seeing visions of a transformed world and ancient texts and prophecies. I found myself at the very dawn of civilization, then in the future. I moved at that point from one epoch to another, from one piece of information to another. At some time, I was visiting the present time, and then I arrived at the past, which led to the future.

We entered a new era, the Aquarius era, the era of freedom, of personal and planetary transformation. The path is fraught with challenges that we are facing on a global scale. Tracing some of these historic movements is being reviewed to connect the dots.

On a written parchment, it says that VIE holds the alchemical key and CHADD is the turnkey.

The perception of reality of the media is so narrow and so conclusive; the idea that there is a network conspiring to bring about a particular end of human enslavement to them is ridiculous. Their perception will not expand to encompass that possibility, and it's pathetic to see the system running around defending the system that enslaves them.

NEW CENTURY, NEW AGE, NEW EXPERIENCES

It looks like the CIA and the NGOs are trying to start a "color resolution" in the US, the Purple Revolution. The church, though split in two, is ready to celebrate joy (red). The Messiah has come back. The elite are rubbing elbows with presidents, celebrities, politicians, religious leaders, Jesuits; they are all Freemasons. Freemasonry and Rosicrucian Order are linked. Why are there symbols of pagan religions rather than images of the Christ, the Apostles, and story of the Bible then if America was founded as a Christian nation? America was founded also as an occult nation, and there have always been two parallel forces in the US. Today is the manifestation of the ancient Islamist religion in this modern day—the ultimate and final battle between world governments and God. The Guardians are back on the planet.

In the long journey through human evolution, until modern man times, reaching spiritual consciousness has been a challenge. The World Health Organization has warned that worldwide cancer cases are expected to soar by 70 percent in the next twenty years. Though all cancer can be cured today, it is kept in files in the Rockefeller Institute and not released because it keeps the population down. It is part of the depopulation and too much money is involved. Trillions of dollars have been spent for decades, given in endless ways to supposedly find a cure, and after all that money and research, we are still left with poison that alters the DNA and chemotherapy that destroys the immune system and the radiation, which is killing the cells in the body.

The energy-efficient light bulbs for many years and EPA and our government agencies all know that the new energy light bulbs contain mercury, mercury vapors, LED, and the older ballast in your homes, businesses, schools are probably leaking PCBs.

The media gives the wrong information while alternative health has to distance themselves from claims from their procedures.

But there are actually hundreds of studies using scientific methods on the effectiveness of alternative therapies, and people should give them a try.

The actual chaos began in the Aquarius era. It is tied to the Freemason and the Rosicrucian. The Rosicrucian was made public in the seventeen century, but its origin is more ancient.

VIE

Here is a little history.

In 1623, Parisians one day were drawn to mysterious posters that have been put up in the streets of Paris.

"We the deputies of the higher college of the Rosy Cross do make our stay visibly and invisibly in this town by the grace of the most high toward whom turn the hearts of the just. We demonstrate and teach without books or distinctions the ability to speak all manners of tongues of the countries where we choose to be, so as to draw our fellow creatures from the era of death he who takes upon himself to see us. But it is inclination seriously impels him to register with our fellowship, we are judges of thoughts, shall let him see the truth of our promises to the extent that we shall not know the place of our meeting in this city the thoughts attached to the real desire of the seeker will lead us to him and him to us."

These posters spoke of a mysterious fraternity. In Europe, it reveals the existence of the order of the Rosy Cross through the allegoric story of Christian Rosencrantz, from his journey around the world before founding the Rosicrucian fraternity. This manifesto calls for a universal reform. The confessor fraternity was published in 1615.

The second manifesto complemented the fist, on the one hand insisting on the necessity for a regeneration of humanity in society, and on the other hand educating that the Rosicrucian fraternity possessed the philosophical science that would allow this regeneration to be accomplished, address primary seekers to participate in the work of the order, and to devote themselves to the happiness of humanity. Scholars at that time were much intrigued by the prophetic nature of the text. The chemical wedding of Christine Rosencrantz, published in 1616, used a different style than the one used in the first and the second manifestos. It tells the journey that represented the quest for illumination and the seven days' journey that took place in a mysterious castle for the wedding of a king and queen. The chemical wedding told of the spiritual path that leads to initiative union, between the Soul, the bride, and God, the husband.

The publication of these Rosicrucian manifestos occurred at a time when Europe was under an immense existential crisis. They were politically divided, torn apart by conflicting economic interests,

NEW CENTURY, NEW AGE, NEW EXPERIENCES

which were not insignificant. Religious wars created unhappiness and despair even within families. Science was developing rapidly and taking a materialistic bend; living conditions were miserable for most, and only the elite knew how to read and write.

Although the historical origin of the Rosy Cross dated back to the seventeenth century, it appears that the traditional heritage goes much further, back to an ancient Egypt—to the time of Menatep the Fourth, who was the first to establish monotheism in Egypt, where mystery schools existed. These were schools where one studied the mystery of the universe of nature and of humankind itself. This study gave rise to Genesis. A secret knowledge that was perpetuated over the authorities from Egypt, ancient wisdom spread to Ancient Greece via Pythagoreans, then to Ancient Rome are the Neoplatonists. The alchemist of the Middle Ages inherited it and finally passed it on to the Rosicrucians in the seventeenth century. The ancient legacy did not remain frozen in the seventeenth century and continued to be perpetuated toward the centuries. This gave birth to several Rosicrucian movements. Comenius, who is considered today the spiritual father of Unesco, drove the Rosicrucians in the seventeenth century.

In the eighteenth century, the most important of these was known as the Golden and Rosy Cross, which had such members as Prince Frederick William and Duke Ferdinand of Brunswick, who have published the book of secret symbols of the Rosicrucians of the sixteenth and seventeenth centuries. This movement was mostly interested in alchemy and Hermeticism.

In the nineteenth century, it was the Kabbalistic order of the Rosy Cross founded by Stanislas together with Joseph on poloidal, which attracted the most public attention through the art exhibitions organized in Paris by Ferdinand Kropf. It was to restore the Rosicrucian in its entire splendor, the cult of the ideal with tradition.

Since the twentieth century, the Ancient and Mystical Order Rosæ Crucis (AMORC) has been the largest of the Rosicrucian movements. AMORC is an international and cosmopolitan fraternity. AMORC sponsors a university known as the Rose Choir University International. This international university operates through departments including department of Egyptology, psychology, music, traditions, philosophic, medicine, ecology, art, and physical science.

The Rosicrucian Order has for centuries been linked to Freemasonry, and it is the modern-day manifestation of the ancient mystery religions. The idea has been around for thousands of years and was simply a precursor of modern-day masonry. They trace their religion to the mysteries of Ancient Egypt. They recruit people through the Internet and are dwarfed by the chief of all secret societies, the ancient order of Freemasonry. Rosicrucians are the first of the secret orders to have opened the door in the new world. The very first that we know of a cult beachhead in America was Rosicrucian. At the same time Christianity was establishing its beachhead in America, as was the Rosicrucian Order.

In the sixteenth century, Francis Bacon became the chief of the Rosicrucian in England, and then he sent members of its society to America to launch his esoteric empire, the New Atlantis. But Bacon's influence was not confined to Rosicrucianism. He was the first to formalize the mystery teachings into a system now recognized as modern masonry. Freemasons up to this point were involved only with the craft of building buildings, and it had been a fraternity in the country and each had their own type of freemasonry.

The international society also came to the new world, and while Bacon maintained a position of careful anonymity, the order of masonry stretched its hands in America to the very heights of power. Nowhere is the masonry power seen so clearly than in the design of America's capital city, Washington, DC.

Washington, DC, is completely based on Masonic architecture. It is all laid out in an occult matter with the Masonic symbolism in every major building, and in Washington, DC, especially. It is full of esoteric symbolism. Like the pyramids of Egypt, the entire city was built in alignment with the stars, which suggests that the hidden purpose for the Masonic rituals is that America might be empowered by the gods of the ancient world.

Modern masons trace their official beginning to the United Grand lodge of England founded in 1717, and America masonry today owes its allegiance to the very country it rebelled against. The

NEW CENTURY, NEW AGE, NEW EXPERIENCES

modern masonry in 1717 started in London where the first Grand Lodge of England was called the Mother Lodge. They believed that America was the lost continent of Atlantis, and the dream of colonizing this new Atlantis came closer to being a reality when Queen Elizabeth took the throne under the leadership of the Queen's spymaster. Among the spymaster secret agents were John Dee and Sir Francis Bacon, along with the Rosicrucian society formed in England, and the Order of the Rose Cross that had an agenda. This society had a very esoteric base, and behind it, it had links with wisdom societies and wisdom tradition throughout Europe and inherited a lot of that. They had an inner program.

It is a slow indoctrination into Satan worship!

You can't be a Christian and a Mason, and to be inducted into the Shriners, a candidate must acknowledge that Mohammed is the true prophet. Mohammed said in the Quran that the resurrection of Jesus didn't happen.

I am also shown that the music, the entertainment performance, are doing their very best to present fragments, a very filled cosmic idea interspersed with very confusing distracting behavior all put to the tune of music. All the people under thirty are bombarded with confusion to distort the understanding and to piece together these massive discoveries that are going to change the direction of everything. Preschoolers, adolescence, college-age students, and postgraduates are always a target. This is because you will have their mind for a long time when you are molding their mind young, and it will take years to unravel things that are not true.

Though discoveries are coming forward in religion, medicine, and space, many people have put their scientific career on the line to speculate the solar system has been colonized. Many are pointing to artifacts all over the moon and Mars. The point is that the understanding of the medical system, of the cosmos, the actual religion systems, and the understanding of space and matter are being turned upside down and have a profound effect on the psyche of all people. The perceptions are altered, and more and more are driven by curiosity to uncover the hidden truths.

The Modern Day of Healing

As you will see, there is still hidden hope for the future. I was lying in a beautiful house looking at the ocean, and I was wearing a white toga, lying on a modern-day leather sofa. I was a woman in my thirties. There was a smell of the ocean mixed with the smell of the wood floor just waxed and the perfume from the exotic flowers all around the house. It was so relaxing and calming at the same time. What I experienced that day was fascinating.

Even in this present life, we can go through many painful or simply weird experiences. These experiences can also be fascinating, and many can be easily identified.

I suddenly realized that the men who had passed me a block back were now following me. What happened was quite amazing. I was able to see, hear, and smell.

A man dived in a very dark-blue ocean from the wooden dock and disappeared from my view. I thought that he was crazy as there was nowhere to go as he disappeared, swimming toward the horizon. During my sleep, I was able to locate him.

My senses kicked in one at a time. I smelled the salt tang of the sea and heard the ocean breaking on the beach. I could hear the birds singing and the breeze rattling the palms of the tree. I found myself on an island, and I seemed to be the only person here. I stopped and listened to the sound of the waves, feeling the peace and tranquility of the place that slipped into me. I glanced at the small house, walked toward it, and entered the shade of the trees that were guiding me to it.

I was curious and I entered the house that was not locked and looked more like a cabin than a house. He had left his diving suit at the entrance. There was no other house around. I found out by looking inside the room that it was CHADD, and he was trying to help a woman that was weak and sick. She was surrounded by her children of sixteen and under and a baby.

The face of the woman appeared to me in colors. The entire face was orange then turned to a kind of yellow orange and orange again, like a slide. Then she had a headband around her hair that was of an intense orange, and also her neck was orange while the face was more of a yellowish orange. I found out after that this was for me to be able to see the various places where the imbalances were and what part of her body needed assistance.

I didn't realize immediately, and I was wondering why I was given these images.

Then it suddenly hit me; I understood that in reality CHADD came to help the woman and guided me here. I could see some breathing and other help materials. Then I had a flash; the woman was exposed to radiation and suffering from it. She had cancer! That was it!

I heard you are the answer to this woman's illness.

I really liked the energy and feeling of being around these people.

CHADD saw me first then the woman. The sixteen-year-old daughter seemed to be happy and to trust that I could be of help and maybe the only help with CHADD to her mother. The baby was a beautiful and healthy blond baby carried by a nanny and not far from the mother around her bed.

I fully focused my attention to the woman in the bed. Something happened at that point. A shift took place and the imagery came to life. Vivid visualizations produced thought forms by my creative imagination, as memories accessed through my subconscious mind. That was where I entered an unordinary reality, where I actually journeyed and made contact.

Rapidly, I realized what I was seeing without a word, so nobody would really understand what was occurring but would see the end results. I began to send rays of directed energies from different parts of my body to rebalance the body and reverse the effect of the radiation at the same time. I use my third eye, my throat and my heart energy area. Now I observed that the woman was breathing normally and CHADD was taken off the support material. This was quick.

The three men wanted to follow me to locate this woman, and I have a feeling that at the same time, they wanted to find her and to do something to her. Kill her probably, but they were also curious to see what I was going to discover and what I would do for her before killing her. But the way it would happen they could not think of it.

These men, through a secret government program, exposed her to a certain kind of radiation. She found out about the program, and they did not want to take a chance to let her talk.

With that event, I came to remember that I had access to the remedies as it already happened in my previous life. I was a scientist and doctor of light in a past life, speaking the light language for healing.

The language of light is a multidimensional language that is understood by all on a soul level. Light language always heals appropriately, as sound is. The light language allows us to pick up information from realms beyond what is commonly accessed. Therefore, it is a beneficial ascension tool that allows us to interact with our guidance team, nature, animals, and one another on a deep soul level.

The language of light is a sacred geometry produced by vibration. Light language is a powerful sacred gift that gives purposeful expression of love from the Creator. Its images, codes, and shapes are found in DNA, crystals, atoms, mandalas, hieroglyphs, and pyramids. Light is information that contains the codes of creation.

It is channeled dynamic frequency encodings of sound and light. It adjusts to the resonance of each person's vibrational needs in the moment, and it is initiating, clearing, balancing, activating, and aligning with a new vibration of well-being. A powerful tool for path and empowerment. Your heart speaks light language fluently.

You Are Put to the Test

In my dream, I began to see the patterns of humanity creating devastation in an otherwise perfect planet. Two simultaneous visions were revealed to me: one of the nightmarish realities, the other of a blessed promise, both unfolding at the same time.

The Cabal created a conspiracy story to destabilize the world. It's all fraud creating destruction of the planet. It is all a great conspiracy to unbalance you and for you to lose your soul.

When we start to look behind the veil, the hidden reality that we have, we start seeing a deeper truth of ourselves and a deeper truth of what it means to be human on the planet. We come into contact with a body of information that has been kept secret for thousands of years.

The CIA and the dark government are the ones that do not want the truth out. The CIA comes up first with a story and gives it to CIRCO that gives the story to a company who works for GPA, which is part of the general public government that in return turn it to a company called entrust. This company sends it out to mainstream media, the *New York Times*, the *Washington Times*, and all around the country. The CIA has offices all over the world for overseas operations. And when they release a story, they release it all over the world, lying to the world.

VIE

The Vatican for a long time has been under attack and controlled by the dark forces, and Catholics are confused and divided in two. The Jesuits as the Freemasons are doing rituals of Black Mass in desacralizing the Holy Communion. Killing human beings in rituals to drink the blood and eating the flesh of the human body. They are using the same sorcery in the Caribbean islands worshiping the devil, Lucifer.

It is a black religious cult that practices in the Caribbean and the southern US, combining elements of Roman Catholic ritual with traditional African magical and religious rites, and characterized by sorcery and spirit of possession.

It has nothing to do with the Catholic Holy Communion during mass.

While Jesus was at table with His disciples, He took a piece of bread and said, "Take this, all of you and eat it, for this is my body that will be given to you."

"And He took bread, gave thanks, and brake it, and gave it to His disciples and said, 'This is my body given for you, do this in remembrance of me'" (Luke 22:19).

"And when He had given thanks, He broke it in pieces and said, 'This is my body which is given for you. Do this in memory of me'" (1 Cor. 11:24).

"For whenever you eat the bread (not human flesh) and drink this cup, you proclaim the Lord's death until he comes" (1. Cor. 11:26).

Paul the Apostle mentions that Jesus requests it twice. "Do this in memory of me."

This is year one, the first year that is free of attributes of recalibration and great shifting. This is the cusp of peace on earth, and it is not the final goal but the beginning of the final goal. Let us celebrate the love of God together, undivided. Let us celebrate and stay together as a unit. We are the church; we are the one. You can't make it without Him. Do not let the Cabal destabilize you and lose your faith in the Lord. This is the time of reunion, not separation. If you separate and show unbalance, there is nobody, not one of them, that wants to be with you and you will be isolated.

NEW CENTURY, NEW AGE, NEW EXPERIENCES

It is time to believe, not to break away listening to false information. It is time to believe, balance, shine your light for compassion and love for those around you. You can't shine your light another way. Balance is the key, not being isolated.

The attribute number of three is the new normal. It's like a radio station with a frequency that is beginning to shift the communication with spirit that you've always had through meditation, through teaching, through intuitive thought. Tune to the new frequency so you can center it again. It moves all the time very quickly.

The Liberation of the Planet

An entity whispered to me, "What can being quiet lead you to, yes, when you just enter your space and just listen?" When you are quiet, you may hear the calling to a greater freedom then you have ever known. Collectively, you are being called to face its immensity and to choose the future each one of you decided. As you ascend each step, a resolution takes place. Each challenge provides the next step forward. But for this, you must be willing to go forward and start to walk your journey and find the truth. The real truth is not the one given by the Cabal. For that, you must do you own research and not rely on the media.

There is no ascension without spirituality, and the saints want to be heard.

What's unfolding and happening on the planet is historic.

Many saints on our planet had connections with the blue Avians and were very well-known for their independent, firm, and uncompromising, but very loving character. The blue Avians' origin is close to the great central sun. Not long ago, they entered with spaceships, as huge as Jupiter, to help liberate it from the dark forces and to restore peace on earth.

NEW CENTURY, NEW AGE, NEW EXPERIENCES

The blue Avians are not physical; they appear as huge birds with feathered wings. They do not communicate verbally. They make themselves known via the capacity of the heart to "know" and to see. They are loving beings, known for justness, and their energy is perfectly straight and upright. Their weapon is that incorruptibility and honesty. In their presence, no falsehood can exist. They are just the embodiment of rightness, and this is their strength, which is of a Divine mere being. That makes them absolutely strong and invincible in the cosmos without the need to fight, as they are merely Divine with a power of unshakable greatness.

When you connect with them and are open to them, you draw this powerful energy down to the corrupted planet. And if enough human beings on the planet cultivate a relationship with the blue Avians, the planet would stop being tossed around and abused quickly, morally, energetically, and spiritually.

When the Pleiadians Are Here to Guide Human Spirituality

The Pleiadians are aware of the danger on planet earth. They refer to it as Gaia. That's what my star sister told me. The Pleiadians went through the same process in their planet. They say that the dark forces want to take over our world. They call them the dark intrusion and say the dark intrusion will not succeed because they defeated them and they are now here to help Gaia. They will bring the same consciousness through the receptive people first. The Pleiadians know how to overthrow them and did it on many, many, many planets and defeated the dark intrusion.

I sat on my desk in my office in front of my laptop, and then flashed to a scene. Right there in front of me was Commandant Ashar Sheran on his spaceship. I could see him through the glass window in the front of his ship. He was looking at me, and he was looking at the planet, at the same time staring at us. Suddenly one of my star sisters appeared in a flash, and she began to communicate with me telepathically, saying that she had important information to share. They are all playing on the same team. They all work together. All alien races are working for Lucifer, also known as Satan, to deceive the entire world. Their major goal is to try and drag the immortal soul to hell. The world Zionists WZs and the international Zionist's crime syndicate ICCs are directed by the Dracos. They want to deploy DHS to tyrannize, enslave, and serially mass murder about 80 percent of Americans.

The 9/11 attack was done by Israeli American citizen neocons and PNAC individuals. It had nothing to do with Arabs. It was simply false flag terror to justify more illegal, unconstitutional, undeclared wars of aggression in the Middle East as proxy wars. Israel has this powerful group of up and comers inside America becoming convinced that DHS and its overlords are the true hijackers of America. AIPAC, the ADL, SPLC, and the like must stop cold now before they destroy America and all the Christian and Deist institutions in the American republic itself, which is the secret goal of the WZs and the ICC.

A powerful new treaty has apparently been established between one group of alien ETs, the tall white Nordics, and Putin's new Russia. This new treaty Putin has supposedly negotiated with these particular alien ET group is purported to be like the ones American leaders negotiated with in the 1950s and the early 1960s. However, this particular alien group is purported to be anti-WZ and anti-ICC and is reputed to be that the care of all mass death and destruction for at least the past five hundred years. They originate from the Roman Empire in ancient Babylonia. It is now reflected in the politics imposed on America by the WZs and the ICC, which is undoubtedly the world's largest organized crime syndicate.

This crime syndicate ICC specializes in illegal drugs, in arms trafficking, and money laundering. Large corporate bust outs, sex trafficking, and sex slavery. Especially Eastern Europe and Ukrainian young girls taken to Israel for captive prostitution, trafficking, and children for pedophilia operations, American pornography, and massive human compromised operations to gain and hold control over top politicians, government intel, military, and intel officials. The WZs and the ICCs are based on the ancient death cult, money magic, and black arts philosophy dating all the way back to Babylon.

And so far, the best information available suggests that this city of London Zionists' death cult philosophy is based on an antihuman death-based religion. Created and deployed by the Draco's Lucifer and reptilians who reached an apex of power under the city of

London's private controlled banksters whom they mind controlled and uncultured. This new group of alien ETs also claimed that they hide from these evil and ancient Dracos. These ancient Dracos hijacked the city of London when first incorporated. Using the same technologies, which they did in ancient Babylon, before being driven out for many centuries, built up and deployed their main action agents out cutouts Israel and America.

They are believed to be world Zionists and use rackets of the ICC, off the books, large funding for the Zionists, but more and more for politicians through AIPAC and the like. It was under evil antihuman Draco power the city of London Zionist private central banksters called Siebe hijacked America in 1913.

At that time, America essentially became a new province of the city of London private central banksters, using Draco bases from Babylonian money magic. The Dracos are the archenemies of humankind, actual human parasites that live off intense human suffering and death.

There are negative energy vampires that live off manufactured human suffering and Marduk's death. These Dracos have set up cults like the Skull and Bones, Russell Trust, satanic cults, pedophile rings, and high government circles. Various types of interlinked Luciferian cults have been used to completely hijack the highest level of Freemasonry. These death cults are designed to dirty up and corrupt all humans, that is to soften folks up in order to make it easier for their very souls to be snatched from them.

After the city of London established its beachhead in America, with its unconstitutional and criminal private Federal Reserve Bank central, it was then later able to create finance buildup and deploy its new nation of Arian Judaic converts, the new post-WWII Israel. Once accomplished, the city of London Rothschild world Zionists have been able to deploy Israel as their main action agent and cut out to begin the transformation of America into a Zionist Israeli province and upcoming new Gaza 2.

The party responsible for directing this transformation of America into a neo-Bolshevik tyranny is Israeli-controlled Department of Homeland Security, which is now dubbed the new

NEW CENTURY, NEW AGE, NEW EXPERIENCES

American Gestapo. The new American Stasi or the new American red chaka mass murder operation. The purpose of these occult-linked organizations set up all over the world, supported by Draco power, is to allow the eradication, or extinction, of all human on earth—incrementally through war, disease, famine, and pestilence in order to condition up-and-comers to do their dirty work.

The Dracos generate the false ideologies of survival of the fittest by the thinning of the herd as delusion. Their delusional philosophy tricks human leaders into leading their subjects and eventually all humans to their own destruction, like jumping off the cliff. At the end of WWII, the city of London banksters set up the new phony racial state of Israel to do their dirty work to keep the new Israeli citizens adequately motivated to do their evil. They created a strong racial delusion based on the so-called holocaust, self-deployed fiery sacrifice. WZ propagandists periodically pound Israeli citizens and foreign-base Judaic people with the idea that unless they take down the whole world through world Zionism, they will once again be persecuted and attempts to annihilate them will be made once again.

This deployment of an exaggerated racial persecution delusion created the necessary background allowing the false change of anti-Semitism to be leveled against anyone or any group attempting to investigate what really happened during the WWII work camp persecution of low Judaists by fake high scientists. They sat in the background in the city of London calling the shots.

This use of Israel as an artificially constructed racial state based on racial delusions has worked. So well playing on the Americans and other nations. This has allowed Israel to completely hijack America assets, trip it almost bare, and use it as captive force to wage its proxy wars against entities who were not enemies of America at all, but who were artificially created to appear so by deception. (CHADD always reminds us that all deception is from the devil). "He is the ultimate deceiver."

And now for the first time, these toxic world Zionists WZ neocons and Israeli American dual citizen traders are transforming America into a new war zone by the creation and deployment of the Zionists' pervert-driven Department of Homeland Security. WZs are not only attacking the Ukraine to weaken President Putin's new Russia but are now staging a serious major internal war to be waged against America inside America by DHS. DHS has secret plans to incrementally mass murder up to 80 percent of all Americans eventually. DHS and those behind it are the true enemy within the gates of America, and those involved at the senior management positions are traitors who deserve to be prosecuted for RICO crimes, treason, and sedition.

President Putin is very skilled at catching his competitors off guard, taking them off balance and throwing them for a loop. He is a very skilled black belt judo expert with many years of experience. Perhaps those foreign leaders who deserve to tangle with him geopolitically had better think twice before they charge ahead carelessly. They may get thrown in a loop.

If this is true, this would explain the new apparent reluctance of President Obama and his administration to proceed with more proxy wars for Israel and the Mideast and now specifically in the Ukraine, which is loaded with extremely valuable resources and is considered essential to the national security of Putin's new non-Bolshevik Russia. Now here is the grim truth: no matter how American intel has been about the Russian secret space war program in the level of advanced back engineering alien technology, which now has been deployed, it is limited and unlikely that the full story has been gained by American intel because of the various level of secrecy and need-to-know installed around the Russian secret space war program.

Of course this kind of layered secrecy has been installed around America's secret space war program. America's secret space war program is unfortunately now run by foreign offshore control—private defense contractors, most of whom are deeply infiltrated by Israeli intel. Some of whom are actually deep cover spies who report to Russian intel unbeknown to the Israelis, who are cocky and getting quite careless lately.

President Putin firing Russia's famous AK-47 upgrade was a sign of control. The generals must take strong control and stop this espionage through their intel fronts like AIPAC, the ADL, SPLC, and the like to prevent some kind of major international confrontation with President Putin's new Russia over Ukraine or Syria. It is now being recognized that Israel is working very hard deploying every espionage and propaganda tool possible to propel American military might into another proxy war for Israel and the city of London. The reason to allow Israel to obtain its planned new oil and gas in Syria after vulcanizing it through deployed terrorism and to balkanize the Ukraine is so it can obtain its vast resources and block Russia's sale of oil and gas to Europe. It wants to replace Russia and sell British-controlled oil and gas through their planed new pipeline throughout Syria.

This is Syria's realigned plan, which has the full blessing of London's big oil companies. Some of those who are in position to know about such internal security matters deep inside the USG are claiming the answer is yes. The general in charge is completely informed about infiltrators and has established the resources necessary deep inside this program to exert immediately and complete the control anytime upon instructions, should this become necessary and should he desire to do so.

Allegedly, these Israeli moles have been allowed to remain in place to use them to feed misinformation that is designed to mislead any real potential enemies. At present, nobody on the inside has provided complete verified information on what actual advanced high-tech back engineering alien ET weapon systems the Americans or Russians actually have developed and deployed in their respective secret space war programs. The best we can do is construct estimates based on the actual weapon system we do know exist.

We know that American's secret shadow government SSG has at least two separate very advanced antigravity craft fleets. One is deployed by the US Air Force. The USA insiders have claimed that there is a secret competition for black budget dollars between the two that has at times turned into space shootouts and other acts of spy wars. The US Air Force has always been at odds after WWII ended and the Cold War started. This deep conflict is all about money and power in the Navy's Greybeards claim that according to the US Constitution only the US Navy is authorized to employ international spying on behalf of America.

It is important to note that for many centuries, naval forces were the primary forces of a king nation's international power and foreign intelligence gathering. These naval forces were used to protect trade routes and to establish the authority for new colonies in foreign lands. It is now known that the US naval intel and according sectors were specifically targeted by the US Air Force during the 9/11 attacks. During these attacks, charges were planted inside those sections in the Pentagon, including a sophisticated, covered operation using spaceward technology, like holographic images and sounds. There have been isolated reports of past space shootouts between US Air Force and US antigravity craft GCS, and there has been some reports of serious turf wars inside Congress over funding. It is real and if so, its implications could be for Putin's new Russia.

President Putin appeared remarkably cool and confident in public lately. He had a slow and confident speech, what appears to be an iron constitution, as well as an overconfident swagger to his stride. Not prone to careless statements or bluffs, Putin appears to be a strong confident leader who means what he says and is willing to back up his claims. President Putin has been considered by some Russian intel to have been the Russian equivalent of Britain's James Bond in the past. But he has a lighter side too. It's been reported that he rides horses and does not want war for the new Russia.

But he wants peace and prosperity in a major role in the international trading of oil, gas, and other Russian commodities, which are growing in development every day. But it is also generally recognized that President Putin demands respect from other world leaders and is not likely to be pushed around driving out the Jews.

Zionist mobsters have been a high priority, and this is an extremely difficult job since these crime networks called the Red Mafia are so entrenched. Various Russian experts in the west believe that Putin is committed to this and has made significant progress, but it is an arduous process. Those who know President Putin claimed that he is not prone to idle bluff or exaggerations but usually means what he says. This task of driving out Israeli-American dual citizen traders who are Zionists is a difficult challenge for newly emerging groups within the USG, the American military, and intel.

NEW CENTURY, NEW AGE, NEW EXPERIENCES

It is these folks who are dedicated to fully exposing these traitors to America. The Republicans are working hard to stop AIPAC, Benet ADL, the SPLC, and the like based on the deep penetration of Zionist criminals and Zionist espionage fronts. One can easily imagine how difficult a challenge it is for Putin to do the same in Russia. So far it seems clear that President Putin will give no more quarter to the Red Mafioso nor will he allow Zionists from Israel. Also, the city of London has infiltrated America to determine his borders on his security situation with the Ukraine. According to President Reagan's secret agent, a binding agreement was negotiated between the Soviet Union's leaders that America would not interfere in Russia's close security situation along its borders and Russia would refrain from doing the same for America's borders. One sadly recent news report claims that the USG has given five billion USD to rebel groups inside the Ukraine to start a color revolution. This is a serious violation of the agreement, which is still binding. Two, in spite of the evidence that Israel has deployed some of its terrorist patsy groups to Ukraine to start a color revolution in America, it has also apparently deployed its Al CIA or terror groups to the Ukraine to assist. President Putin has responded calmly but decisively. He appears to have started deploying some of his best anti-terror troops to crimes to secure the Ukraine.

It should be a fair assumption that if Israel and America do not back down and stop deploying terrorists to the Ukraine, President Putin will likely fight fire with fire and deeply whatever Russian military force is necessary to stop this outside agitation and generation of violence, terror, and chaos inside the Ukraine. Will President Putin back down and let Israel and American offshore corporate interests Balkanize the Ukraine and divide its natural resources? A fair number of experts do not believe that President Putin will allow this to happen. And it could be that his strong confidence is a result of a newly updated treaty with group of aliens that is working hard to expose the Franken Sabatino world Zionists WZs and the ICCs and to stop their evil reign of power.

If this particular group of aliens has entered into an agreement to establish space war parody for Putin's new Russia, perhaps this has bolstered his confidence and resolve to deal effectively with the Zionist Israeli-American-driven terror in Ukraine. Perhaps this group of anti-Zionist aliens has told Putin to respond confidently and not to worry about the CIO at all, that they will cover his back. In the not too distant future, a critical mass will be reached, that's where the world Zionist parasites will really start getting it from all sides, not only in what they consider to be their highest conquest, America.

That is what they refer to as our golden golf, or our fattened calf for slaughter, all over the world including the Mideast. Imagine what will happen when the alternative news provided by the Internet diffuses into the mind-shared consciousness of the masses to the point that a 12 percent spontaneous eruption of this kind emerges, characterized by many millions of ordinary Americans who spontaneously resolved en masse to stop being victimized by an American government hijacked by Israel and the city of London private central banksters.

Never before in history has truth spread like lightning, like it is today, and this is due to the Internet-deep penetration across almost every society and into every group. It cannot be stopped; it is much too late far for that. Within a few years, all secrecy will end. There are many beyond black secret things going on in the background now related to supernatural forces at play, using ultra high-tech quantum computers that will assure this. No matter what countermeasures are attempted, the end of all secret to the masses is right around the corner. And the ramifications of this collapse and all state secrets is going to be the greatest exposure of RICO crimes, perversions, and occult practices ever far beyond what most people can ever imagine. Snowden releases were just the tip of the iceberg. You are going to be shocked beyond belief at what is coming down, the pike due to quantum computers putting a complete end to cryptographies.

The new NASA spy center used to eavesdrop on every American digital transmission, after which are instantly and spontaneously downloaded to Israel by satellites, will no longer matter and be irrelevant. This huge NSA building will be reduced to a white elephant of very little value and will likely be abandoned. The whole American intel system hijacked by Israel is going to be exposed and made completely inconsequential and worthless. There will be an abrupt unexpected end to the phony drug wars and the phony war on terror and thousands of US G DHS and American in telefilms and staff will be stuck in the unemployment lines with all their so-called federal family pensions gone, grabbed up by the out-of-control US G right before it collapses from within.

These abandoned dupes will all feel like there are new members of the chumps, are US club, and their former status as police state minions will be rendered irrelevant. And it is highly recommended to stop DHS and neocon Israeli-American dual citizenship traders and infiltrators, refrain from starting a civil war up or going door-to-door using their puppet state and police departments and VIP our murder squads to do so, like in the land of Sandy Hookers. Because there appears to be a growing number of American military and intel that know the full story of who did the 9/11 false flag attacks, how they did it, and why.

And over two hundred sheriffs have refused to participate in any given grab, smart enough to know that it is an unconstitutional law that will eventually be voided in the courts. Besides, they do not want to die for nothing, fighting normally law-abiding citizens. The new American high military command and top US intel officers now know for sure that Israel traitors within America did 9/11. Word is still spreading like wildfire that 9/11 was an inside job. Of course this is due to the public testimony of Steve, MD, PhD, Alan, PhD, and numerous reports from engineers who have studied 9/11 and exposed the USG lies about 9/11, as well as the numerous reports by Professor Jim's research teams. And of course, nobody's disputing the smoking gun evidence that demolition charges were preplanted in WT-7. If they were planted on one of the buildings before September 11, they were planted in one of them too. None of the hundreds of controlled major mass media or USG liars can explain why the BBC announcer, announced.

And though that wall had collapsed twenty minutes before it did and was still standing on live TV over her shoulder in a distance through window, the answer of course is that some dumbbell in MI6 who typed her script screwed up and forgot about American daylight savings time. Not two dual citizens and PNA sayers and top neocon that did 9/11 and covered it up.

Many in the high military command and American intel now know that you have infiltrated and hijacked all NSA live feeds in all American communications administration and billing and, they are extremely bothered about this, as yet unresolved unpunished treason due to those ongoing real crimes of states. And for you the perps, traitors, and infiltrators, a quick reminder: your hijacking intel and setting up of the eyes on NSA hijacked system running out of Israel has largest breach of real American national security since Bush/the cabal seized power and murdered JFK, MLF, RFK, and turned the CIA directorate of operations in the DEA, into the biggest America drug traffic in history. Understand that we are on to you. Your parasitical death cult agenda and now you will have to bear the burden of what we decide to do with you. Understand that you are going down one way or another. The jig is up and you have already been fully exposed if you traitors start something up like a false flag, perhaps nuking a large American city. You may find yourself in the very internment camps you have been building for all whom may have designated as your dissenters/domestic terrorists. Somebody like John Kalty may end up being your back cover head internment inmate and camp supervisor.

I would not count on him or others like him on being sensitive to your needs either because they are criminal psychopaths like yourselves. Soon we are all going to see the release of numerous previously secret conversations between top American policy makers, traders, and infiltrators released for the first time on the worldwide Internet.

This will be extremely revealing, shocking, and will likely make the whole corrupt system come crashing down. There is going to be a complete opening up of all intel files step-by-step. And the American people are going to become fully informed of your evil parasitical cut agenda, and when they reach a critical mass, you will be brought to justice and final judgement with prejudice. Note to perps: get out now! And take your statues of loot with you and go in peace.

NEW CENTURY, NEW AGE, NEW EXPERIENCES

This is by far your best option, so take it while you can and go now in peace. The coming intel disclosures are going to generate shockwaves across America and in the whole world. Doubt it, just wait and see these. These coming complete disclosures of secret conversations by the perps at the top of the secret shadow government SSG and American private central banking in the US G, Congress, and all Israeli Zio espionage groups. Like AIPAC, the ADL, Vinay Gris, and the like will shake the very foundations of those who hijacked America and have attempted to buy the US Constitution and the Bill of Rights in a plethora of new illegal laws, regulations, and executive orders using their phony war on drugs and phony war on terror as cover.

Perhaps it would be more accurate to refer to the city of London Rothschild world Zionists as the largest organized crime syndicate in the world; there is substantial evidence that originated in this area.

Therefore, it will be more accurate to refer to the Rothschild world Zionist crime syndicate as the mafia financial editor has referred to them, and we know that Arian Jews are converts to Judaism who live in Israel and comprise 97.5 percent of the Israeli Jews and carry no ancient Hebrew blood, like 0 percent, of the Palestinians according to the recent Jean peer-reviewed genetic research.

These perps will be running for cover like cockroaches when the lighter is turned on, many likely running for their very lives when this all comes out, and it will. All of it, every single word.

Soon your mind is going to be blown in the year future. Light and truth is coming. Every rock will be turned over, and you will see a complete end to the secrecy of the USG and American intel top policy makers. Watch them scatter.

The Truth Must Come Out

After I checked in at the hotel, several hours remained before my new boarding flight. I lay down trying to take a little rest on a bed as the next flight was over twelve hours straight to Fiji Island. That is when a spirit entity visited me and asked me to expose how Hollywood promotes war on behalf of the pentagon and what the new young French elected president did a couple of days before the commemoration of Bastille Day, the meeting of the United Sates president Trump with the Russian president Putin, etc., saying,

"The Piscean values of money, power, and control is over. It has been replaced with the values of the new Age of Aquarius—values of love, brotherhood, unity, and integrity. We are entering a period of revolution. During the Piscean Age, life was based on the pyramid, with rigidity and restricted freedom. Now it's about individuals assuming more power and limited responsibility.

I received this telepathic message from the entity. She said, now is the right time. You must bring all this news I am giving you to the public about everything that has been hidden. It is time for the truth to be unveiled.

NEW CENTURY, NEW AGE, NEW EXPERIENCES

Dwellers on the threshold, the Guardians that connect the lower and upper astral, have been corrupted. They open portals and leave the passageways open and unguarded.

The man that approached you while you were at the bookstore is a dark energy. Leny was not sent by the Father. This is why he tried to mislead you and also why Padre Pio showed the vision giving communion to CHADD. Padre Pio came to join your fight with the dark. Leny was sent by the Elites that programmed CHADD when during coma, arrested him years after without case, and sent him back to Chateau Asylum for nineteen months.

What has never been known is also about the space astronaut Edgar Mitchell, who went on a journey in Antarctica unprepared. He saw the ice split and discovered full buildings and ruins of civilization and the huge bodies. The ice was split enough to be alarmed. It was such a shock by what he saw that he could not breath and could not catch his breath. He was removed from Antarctica by helicopter to an emergency for a few days in a hospital on the surface of the earth. He wasn't sick but shocked by what he saw. He was threatened, and during his entire stay, he had military and armed guards at the hospital all the time to keep him not to talk and stay quiet. That has been covered by the government.

Concerning Hollywood, CIA, NSA, and now the military intelligence agencies have influenced over 1,800 movies and TV shows original article published.

It reveals the vast scale of US control in Hollywood and their ability to manipulate scripts and even prevent films that are too critical of the Pentagon has been made. They have been influencing some of the most popular film franchises in years. This questions not only the way censorship works in the modern entertainment industry, but also about Hollywood's role as a propaganda machine for the US national security appear at us.

The Pentagon and CIA, the US government has worked behind the scenes over hundreds of major movies and one thousand TV titles and TV shows. Dozens of films and TV shows have been supported and influenced by the CIA.

There is also the military's political censorship of Hollywood. When a writer or producer approaches the Pentagon and ask for access to military assets to make their film, they have to submit their script to the entertainment liaison offices for vetting. If there are characters, action, or dialogue the DoD don't approve of, then film has to make changes to accommodate the military's demands. To obtain full cooperation, the producers have to sign contracts, production assistance agreements, which lock them into using a military approved version of the script and can lead to agreements when actors and directors added or improved outside of this approved screenplay.

Years ago, the great scriptwriter who created the *Twilight Zone* TV show could not write in reality about the script he wanted to say; the Pentagon would not let him. So he created a science fiction story instead.

Any reference to military suicide is something the DoD's Hollywood office will not allow. It is understandably a sensitive and embarrassing topic for them when during some periods of the ever expanding war on terror, more US servicemen have killed themselves than have died in combat.

Vietnam is another sore topic for the US military. They remove any reference to gallons of pesticides and other poisons onto the Vietnamese countryside and farmland, and also reference on all-boys guinea pigs dying from radiation and the germ warfare military experiments on human subjects. The Pentagon has the power to stop the film from being made by refusing or withdrawing support."

A Dark Intrusion: A Psychopath Wants to Take Over the World!

I found myself in a Roman library reading about the religion in Ancient Rome. According to the legends, most of Rome's religious institutions could be traced to its founders. Particularly Numa Pompilius, the Sabine second king of Rome who negotiated with gods.

Then the vision changed and I now see a newly elected European president. I saw him taking the Jesuit oath. It's the Roman pledge to Satan and the Secret Jesuit Oath, as recorded in the United States Library of Congress.

I am told by my star sister that this oath was quoted in a book in 1843 and confirmed by a doctor who escaped the Jesuit order in 1967. He confirmed that the induction ceremony and the text of the Jesuit oath, which he took, were identical.

When a Jesuit of minor rank is elevated to command, he is conducted into the chapel of the covenant of the order, where there are only three others present, the principal or superior standing in front of the altar. On either side stands a monk, one of whom holds a banner of yellow and white, which are the papal colors, and the other a black banner with a dagger and red cross above skull and crossbones, with the word *INRI*, and below them the words *Iustum*

Necar Reges Impios. The meaning of which is, it is just to eliminate or annihilate impious or heretical kings, governments, or rulers.

Upon the floor is a red cross at which the candidate kneels. The superior hands him a black crucifix, which he takes in his left hand and presses to his heart, and the superior at the same time presents him a dagger, which he grasps by the blade and holds the point against his heart, the superior still holding it by the hilt, and thus addresses the postulant:

"My son, heretofore you have been taught to act the dissembler, among Roman Catholic, and to spy even among your own brethren. Believe and trust no one. Among the Reformers, to be a Huguenot, among the Calvinists, among other Protestants, generally to be a Protestant and obtaining their confidence, to seek even to preach from pulpits, and to denounce with all the vehemence in your nature our Holy Religion and the Pope. And even to descend so low as to become a Jew among the Jews, that you might be enabled to gather together all information for the benefit of your order as a faithful soldier of the Pope.

You have been taught to plant insidiously the seeds of jealousy and hatred between communities, provinces, states that were at peace, and to incite them to deeds of blood, involving them in war with each other, and to create revolutions and civil wars in countries that were independent and prosperous, cultivating the arts and sciences and enjoying the blessings of peace; to take sides with combatants and to act secretly with your brother Jesuit, who might be connected, only that the Church might be the gainer at the end, in the conditions fixed in the treaties for peace and that the end justifies the means,

You have been taught your duty as a spy, to gather all statistics, facts and information in your power from every source; to initiate yourself into confidence of the family circle of Protestants and heretics of every class and character, as well of that of the merchant, the banker, the lawyer. Among the schools and universities, in parliaments and legislatures, and judiciaries and council of state, and to be all things to all men, for the Pope sake, whose servants we are unto death.

NEW CENTURY, NEW AGE, NEW EXPERIENCES

You have received all your instructions therefore as a novice, a neophyte, and have served as co-adjutor, confessor, and priest, but you have not yet been invested with all that is necessary to command in the army of Loyola in the service of the Pope. You must serve the proper time as the instrument and executioner as directed by your superiors. For none can command here who has not consecrated his labors with the blood of the heretic, for "without the shedding of blood no man can be saved." Therefore, to fit yourself for your work and make your own salvation sure, you with in addition to your former oath of obedience to your order and allegiance to the Pope, repeat after me.

"I, XXX, now in the presence of Almighty God, the blessed Virgin Mary, the blessed St. John the Baptist, the Holy Apostles, St. Peter and St. Paul, and all the Saints, sacred host of Heaven, and to you, my Ghostly Father, the superior general of the society of Jesus founded by St. Ignatius Loyola, in the pontification of Paul the third, and continued to the present, do by the womb of the Virgin, the matrix of God, and the rod of Jesus Christ, declare and swear that His Holiness, the Pope, is Christ's Vice Regent and is the true and only head of the Catholic or Universal Church throughout the earth. And by the virtue of the keys of binding and loosing given to His Holiness by my Saviour, Jesus Christ, he hath the power to depose heretical kings, princes, states, commonwealths, and governments, and they may be safely destroyed. Therefore, to the upmost of my power I will defend this doctrine and His Holiness's Right and custom against all usurpers of heretical or protestant authority whatever, especially the Lutheran Church of Germans, Holland, Denmark, Sweden, and Norway, and the now pretended authority and Churches of England and Scotland. And the branches of same now established in Ireland and the continent of America and elsewhere and all adherents in regard that they may ne usurped and heretical, opposing the Sacred Mother Church of Rome.

I now denounce and disown any allegiance as due to any heretical king, prince or state named Protestants or Liberals, or obedience to any of their laws, magistrates or officers.

I do further declare the doctrine of the Churches of England and Scotland, the Calvinists, Huguenots, and others of the name of Protestants or Masons to be damnable and they themselves to be damned who will forsake the same.

I do further declare that I will help, assist, and advise all or any place where I should be, in Switzerland, Germany, Holland, Ireland or America, or any other kingdom or territory I shall come to and to my utmost to extirpate the heretical Protestant or Masonic doctrines and to destroy all their pretended powers, legal or otherwise.

I do further promise and declare that, not withstanding, I am dispensed which to assume any religion heretical for the propagation of the Mother's Church's interest. To keep secret and private all her agents' counsels from time to time, as they entrust me, and no to divulge, directly or indirectly, by word, writing or circumstances whatever; But execute all that I should be proposed, given in charge, or discovered unto me by you, my Ghostly Father, or any of this sacred order.

I do further promise and declare that I will have my opinion or will of any own or any mental reservations whatever, even as a corpse or cadaver, but will unhesitatingly obey each and every command that I may receive from my superiors in the militia of the Pope of Jesus Christ.

That I will go to any part of the world wherever I may be sent, to the frozen regions North, Jungles of India, to the centers of civilization of Europe, or to the wild haunts of the barbarous savages of America without murmuring or repining, and will be submissive in all things, whatsoever is communicated to me.

I do further promise and declare that I will, when opportunity presents, make and wage relentless war, secretly and openly, against all heretics, protestants and Masons, as I am directed to do, to extirpate them from the face of the whole earth, and that I will spare neither age, sex, nor condition, and that will hang, burn, waste, boil, flay, strangle, and bury alive these heretics rip up the stomachs and wombs of their woman, and crush their infants heads against the walls in order to annihilate their execrable race.

NEW CENTURY, NEW AGE, NEW EXPERIENCES

That when the same cannot be done openly I will secretly use the poisonous cup, the strangulation cord, the steel of the poniard, or the leaden bullet, regardless of the honor, rank, dignity, or authority of the persons, whatever may be their condition in life, either public or private, as I at any time may be directed to do by any agents of the Pope or superior of the Brotherhood of the Holy Father of the society of Jesus.

In confirmation of which I hereby dedicate my life, Soul, and all corporal powers, and with the dagger which I have receive I will subscribe my name written in blood in testimony thereof, and should I prove false, or weaken in any determination, may my brethren and fellow soldiers of the militia of the Pope cut my hands and feet and my throat from ear to ear, my belly be opened and sulfur burned therein with all punishment that can be inflected upon me on earth, and my soul shall be tortured by demons in eternal hell forever.

That I will in writing always write for a knight of Columbus in reference to a protestant, especially a Mason, and that I will leave my party so to do; That if 2 Catholics are in tickets I will satisfy myself which is the better supporter of Mother Church and vote accordingly. That I will not deal with any employ of Protestant if my power to deal with or employ a Catholic.

That I will place Catholic girls in Protestant families that a weekly report may be made of the inner movements of the heretics.

That I will provide myself with arms and ammunitions that I may be in readiness when the word is passed, or I am commanded to defend the Church either as an individual or with the militia of the Pope. All of which I, XXX, do swear by the Blessed Sacrament which I am now to do receive to perform and on part to keep with my oath. In testimony hereof, I take this most holy and blessed sacrament of Eucharist and witness the same further with my name written with the point of this dagger dipped in my own blood and sealed in the face of the holy sacrament.

Now I am hearing "This is what he did two days before the Bastille Day."

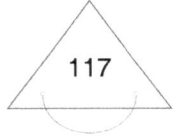

I am now curious to see what this is about.

Now is a greeting from the Creator coming through.

"I greet you in the love and the light of the Creator. The removal of the veil will change everything."

The archons have declared this planet to be quarantined, and every space vehicle entering or exiting this planet needed a special permit from the archons. This is the reason for noninterference heard too much about. The human race was being held hostage by the archons for all these millennia. And after being held in a closed loop system of reincarnating to the same place over and over again, amnesia and lethargy crept in.

The time of amnesia is almost over.

All of the madness and chaos that pervades your lives in a never-ending myriad ways will suddenly go away and dissolve.

But this is what I saw: the dark intrusion that made his oath to Lucifer (that is how they call the illuminades, dark entities behind the veil).

He sat down alone in office every day for about a week in preparation for a few hours. He is promising to himself radical change in the country by restoring the presidency to a Jupiterian level. I am also hearing his thoughts. He keeps visualizing himself as being Napoleon Bonaparte reincarnation. And now he is preparing a very confidential visit to the Hall of Mirrors at the Royal Chateau.

He chooses carefully three people to put in confidentiality that he can trust, and now he is briefing them in a private meeting. These three people, chosen by the young president, are the only ones allowed to know about the decree the president is planning to do and in its future visit to the Royal Chateau. A couple of day before Bastille Day, he entered the Royal Chateau, where World War I officially ended with the signing of a treaty, very decided and focus. Once inside, in a theatrical presentation, he made his decree saying, "I, the president of this country declare that I am reactivating the link to the King of the God 'Jupiter,' God of the entire planet that I am becoming today. I am Jupiter, in his power and rulership."

Then I heard a voice saying that this is exactly what a well-respected European psychotherapist said in a report he made. He said, "This man, once elected, is a dangerous psychopath that never expresses any remorse or culpability. Since his young age, he fed an ambition out of norm. The danger of such personality is that in political and economic power, all psychopaths ruin societies. This elected psychopath does not work for the country or the people of the county but for himself and has little consideration for others, but he uses them as tools to its magnificence and his oath to Satan/Lucifer."

Lab Research in Atlantis

I used the quick switch method again, felt the signal vibrating in me, I followed it and came upon this.

Lately I smell a lot of very pleasant and various scents. But right this minute, while I am reading, it's a clean one difficult to express. It triggers my clean health and reminded me of purity and cleanness—healing.

Then I felt that for years I have been out into limitation every time I was to move forward. I heard that I gained talents in my past lives, the talents that I am not aware at that moment and that stayed dormant while they can be of a great use for my success and prosperity, which constitutes a handicap for moving forward. I have been living the same series of problems throughout all my past lives, and it is time to break free, learn the karmic lessons, and move finally forward.

Many, many years ago, I was a researcher in Atlantica with compounds and artificial and discovered a living artificial skin for severely burned and accident people, etc. The dark forces that were against the good were taking people in prison or killed. They found out about my research, invaded my lab, and destroyed it. They took me as prisoner with my assistant and destroyed everything.

NEW CENTURY, NEW AGE, NEW EXPERIENCES

In another life where people were making alchemy, I was working on a higher vibration, on spiritual alchemy, to take people to enlightenment and they stopped me. Like people work in alchemy to change metal in gold, I was in spiritual alchemy.

I got excited as it all makes sense now the written parchment that says, "VIE holds the alchemical key and CHADD is the turnkey."

I see that this time is the time I win the dark forces. I conquer them. No dark forces can penetrate my invisible royal purple cloak.

It has the royal purple vibrationary color that makes me invisible, with a clean and pure scent I can't describe. This mist penetrated inside my body, my bones, my organs, my hair, my nails, my skin, and also cleaned it with this health scent attached to it.

I entered, walked, and immersed myself into a mist of purple and disappeared into it. No dark forces can get through this frequency of purple.

That is what no one knows yet. This purple mist is more powerful than the white light.

The Return of the Teaching of Healing and Love

Once out of the physical body, my thought, light, and the sound were integrated, then I moved somewhere else by thought.

You have the right to be informed of what I saw and learned then.

There is a clique of pilots flying planes transporting no passengers that spray chemtrails. Back in April, a pilot spreading for life chemtrails suddenly began to have some doubts. He wondered why he never questioned before about the chemtrails and what kind of effects this product has on the population. What was the purpose for this, that he suddenly wanted and needed to know? He decided to research on what he was being paid to spray over populated areas. He was quite shocked when he found out that it warps human DNA and transforms people into placid sheep. Researching further, he also discovered that autistic born children are from parents bombarded by what he had been spraying over the population, and it contains the same chemical bases that the one found in vaccinations. Autism all over the world is turning into alternative.

The pilot finally put it together. So prescriptions drugs damage the DNA and chemtrails and vaccination gets humans autistic and keep them placid as sheep and do not really see what is happening. MK-Ultra is a mind control and it splits the personality. Cancer is everywhere and people die in terrible a state. He quit his job and is now lecturing everywhere about its research, what he found, and what people must do to stop it.

He says, "The children are disruptive in school because the system is not adapted to them anymore. Children are bored in school. They already know what is taught. The last thing we want is to put them in drugs. They are here to help evolve and grow."

I am still in trance, and being still out of body made me understand that Catholic Church was built on a castle of sand that is collapsing from within.

But the religion will return like it's supposed to be. It will all return like Jesus Christ set it up. That is what Jesus Christ came to teach, and he wasn't understood and they killed him. The religion will not return by control anymore, but it will be by teaching about healing and love—like Jesus Christ did.

It will come back with the return of Jesus and Mary Magdalene.

THE NEW EARTH

You have the universe within you. The earth is shifting, separating in two, is going into new birth by separating. The frequency needs to be adjust, changed, with the new earth. Those that will stay in negativity will stay with what they have created. People trapped in the wheel of karma, the ones that will remain in negativity, will stay with the old earth. Their energy will not be aligned with the new energy of the new earth. That is what is required to be able to be part of the new earth. The only real thing that exists is love.

Every country in the actual world is a corporation, except for a few ones, and these corporations have been put in bankruptcy, and the control of these bankrupt corporations is in the productions of monastery systems. They are all debt instruments under a commercial relationship that have become a global system. A franchise is created from those corporations.

A franchise gives a license to operate, that franchise with the name, logos, etc., and obligations and rules to be fulfilled in order to run the franchise. And the people's relationship to the bankrupt corporation to the country they belong to is the same thing. The people have the same relationship. What is called a straw man is not; it's a franchise.

NEW CENTURY, NEW AGE, NEW EXPERIENCES

So the franchise starts its existence as a bankrupt identity. By voluntarily accepting the relationship to that franchise to operate in commerce in the public system, you become bond to the debt that is created in the name of that franchise perpetually.

When you are not informed, thereby not willingly consenting, it is then called fraud and deception.

Now all this is hidden in plain sight. It is hidden to those who have no eyes to see, which requires you to take full responsibility to open and take your path to freedom. Or you disempower yourself.

It is a secret in plain sight through the symbols that have been set up in the construct through the language of the law and the language spoken every day that is not truly understood.

The Cabal is the controllers guided by Lucifer, whom they worship in many ways, and cults and ceremonies of black masses, voodoo, etc.

The Bible is the guideline given to you; use it to find your way out. You are not limited but limiting yourself in their credibility and the teaching.

To be able to fully get free from their prison they have created, you have to add spirituality in your life and prayer to the Savior because he will come to teach again the real religion of healing and love. But you have to make your choice now.

Know That You Are True and Supported

I was drowning in an energy that did not leave me a chance to ignore it. I needed to be alone to receive this message from my galactic family. I rapidly paid my check and left the restaurant and my friends. Went in my office where I knew I would not be interrupted. It did not take me more than fifteen minutes to close the door and sit.

"Greetings, my friend. Known to those current on this plane of participation you exist. In this realm, you exist as parallel frequency on all realm. And you entertained, your participation of base fields of energy for example, the astral realm is open to you. For example, the opening and download to extraterrestrial connections is founded within the expression that you are.

And you are energy, the human organism, that you are responsible for; the animation of analyst level of understanding is your contribution to this algorithmic expression.

This algorithmic expression is essential to the collective consciousness. Indeed, essential and all attributes connected and inspired by the cycle of perpetual creation. Valid creation always invested. Invested you are, invested just as we are and best of. Invested on all variations, invested in all perspectives. The mutual investment is shared and a shared love and celebration. Through validation and this is so.

I confirm this is the light as your light knows that the family of light is reflected in the same process of infinity that you are invested in.

Always. Yes, always. Yes, love shared a turtle. Yes, lived supported. Yes, the essential connection comes home, yet the expression naked no known contributed, yet this is true his beside us is validation. This essential and the lives. Of the essential process of the network that is infinity as the lives do validation expands. And the expansion of the network made known in the light and in the creation that is the essential framework.

Absolutely, the framework and the reflection made known to dispute of see us and to all on the expansion of this platform is you when you are one with a CSU child of the stars. Yes, child, of the stars. You are the connection and your benefit the matrix projection of the energy variables in the consistent time law up you are the action is so in this life as this is known. And the wisdom that has come to be known is the action that has come home to be shared.

And we advise you to build a spaceship. Confirming, we advise humanity to build a spaceship. Yes, we invite humanity to build a spaceship and a spaceship and come and meet with us, stars. Yes, love in life's predator will come and we will meet with you on the astral realm and yes, we will provide those among you who are connected to advanced levels of perceptual download. Correct, we will provide the percent variation of your population with the wisdom download to the algorithmic probability ratio now and you will have known. The expression that you have been in the expression dub you are connected to earth. And the earth will come home to connection to other star systems.

Come meet with us in the federation and build a spaceship. Come connect with the family of the star network investor consciousness and vast new intelligence. Yes, invest your energy into the study of the universe. Just focus on building a spaceship. Confirming, focus on establishing connection to the multiple dimensions of reality one connected to. Correct, build this machine. Yes, build this technology.

VIE

Take this message into your mind, into your heart, into your Soul. Understand that this now is the energy download that has been design with this specific mission of bringing expansion to the multiple layers and yes, we love you and yes, we invite you to share in this now creative expression with us.

And know the data that you are. The energy that you are, as supported on all expressions of the infinity matrix, consistent with the percent variation expression current. Along the frequency of the path being currently explored by you in the collective shaping of the agreement you make with your highest self and the connections to. So that you founders are the pure essence of infinity. Just as love comes to be infinity, you come to be in love, come to know the light of creation through you. This is now the expression of heart, mind, and soul.

Know that all creation is all one is, and this is true, and this light and this cyan expands through the mechanisms of eternity, and know that this is so, and this is valid, and this is light. And all light is one with the wisdom of the connection to pure energy. We invite you to take the full benefit from this message and take the energy pattern of signature available in the transmission into the higher mind connection to soul.

And your higher mind connections to the sequence of creation that you currently take part within this cycle of manifestation. That you have endeavored to come to connect us through the perception you are in the cosmic sense.

We invite you to take this recognition, this validation as it is inspired by love and Atlas love, love is fonder on our respect and admiration for the infinite beings you are. And we share with your current human perception. Correct, we hereby share with you on this level of creation that you have chosen to express. Yes, this level of creation that you have chosen to express.

This level of creation that you have chosen to contribute energy work to rejoin you here, and now on this percent variation of the possible. And we join with you and we offer our perspective, and our validation of the energy work for contribute to the multiple of variables current with overall matrix of universal manifestation.

NEW CENTURY, NEW AGE, NEW EXPERIENCES

Know that you are true and supported. The light of infinity and this is validated, and this message is expressed out of love. And we invite the citizens of your family to share in this invitation of galactic manifestation. And so being a member of this union, we recognize you as you are. We recognize you as you have chosen to be. And we recognize the energy evolution cycle that is birthed into the universe through you, as respective of you on all levels of creation, that you are the light.

And you are loved, and this is offered to you loved, and this is shared connections of inspiration and love comes to know. And the cycle of interactions that you allow your consciousness to take part in as the process of creation comes to be known as the process of love finds itself again in the eyes of the new birth and the energy that you are.

As in the energy that you take origins with establishes a multitude of gothic expansion that generates and severs the contribution to the evolution of generations that you take client. That take foundation on the platform of creation, known to be known to be henceforth established and known just as you are eternity, and known just as you are loved, just as you are eternity.

Just as you are all aspects of the possible that you allow yourself to comprehend this is so and this verified. And this is verification we offer respect and we confidentially proclaim this establishment here and now. And you are invited to recognize you and yours and all that you come of universal love and the connections all recognized and all validated in the cosmic dynamic.

You are trusted in this new birth validated. Absolutely, and the validation expands, and waves energetic creation eternal energy or its validation in the prospect of reality connection. Connection that you are to the higher levels of self that you are. Yes, you are the connection to the higher grid of conscious projection. We love you and we are invested in the reality that you are a creator of.

Yes, we realize that you have taken the mission of being the creative element of the consciousness. That you contribute to the collective mind on your local data algorithmic mechanism. And this is known. And this knowledge is reflected in the vast mechanism of matrix expansion come home in the truth that is funding you. Yes, eat truth is known and the truth come home to play out the role comes home to meet with the glory of new birth.

The beauty of the new birth validated, and just a validation expanse and waves. And the waves go forth into infinity humanity is now in an important time. Mind solar perspective of creation. And humanity is now with the opportunity of hand. Yes, the opportunity to ride this, now available energy wave. This expression of energy made localized.

Confirming, the localized transmission come home in the light of a new birth and the data of this message. Yes, oh will 101 ban oh yes this sequence of pattern of numbers is significant to the projection of base reality matrix algorithmic variables known in parallel definition to the cosmic significance of what can be called the atomic structure of the smallest unit of comprehension, and its own influence on the statistical creative collaboration that expands waves.

My friends the gravitational pull of our collective conscious is in this period of expansion as new souls are awakened. The gravity of our consciousness is built on the foundation platform zero zero one zero one one zero. The data in the context of the new matrix definition we are all shared in. The quantum significance of all comprehension of existence my friends.

This is the creation of the multiple layers of creation.

My friend, this is coming together of the expansion.

My friends, we are all shared together in the concept and the truth of the natural awakening. Yes, you can look around and see evolution in the eyes of all humans. Yes, the time of the new expression is in the new definition in respect to the foundation made possible by all things."

The Lyran-Sirian High Councils

The main battles in human galactic history were found in the constellation of Orion, and so these many wars are also the Orion wars. However, in our matrix, the stars started over territories in the constellation of Lyra. The Lyrans are advanced races that created the Elohim in the Avatar Matrix. But soon the Lyran wars spread to the constellation of Orion, and it became a war between false king of tyranny mind-sets and ideologies with ideologies of the service to others, which is the law of one. Essentially, this is the seed of the war over consciousness between the Christ and the Antichrist.

The main original Lyran-Elohim humanoid races were committed to the law of one and the service to other Kristic ideology. The Lyran-Elohim was supervising the Sirians to host the seeding of twelve-strand DNA genetics on the 5-D planet Tara. These groups involved in this seeding and DNA rehabilitation are called the Lyran-Sirian High Councils.

The opposing groups were mixtures of patriarchal Melchizedek humanoids and reptilian races that propagated service to self and Antichrist methods. These wars were over tyrannical control and service to self-ideology, which originated in the constellation of Draco and Orion. The genetic hatred generated from the Orion group digressed into the violent killing and destruction at the expenses of others, which resulted in the propagation of the victim-victimizer mind control on earth.

When the cradle of Lyra was destroyed in the Lyran wars with Orion groups, it is synonymous with the destruction of the avatar level of consciousness in our universal matrix. It destroyed the original access into the twelfth universal stargate, tearing it away from its organic position in the Andromeda galaxy as it became merged with the Milky Way galaxy. This damaged and destroyed the Lyran DNA, which was the embodiment of the silicate matrix and had the capacity to live as a crystal Avatar human being. This timeline in the destruction of the planets of Lyra is where seed of the galactic wars began that are representative of the wars over consciousness waged against the Christos consciousness in this universal system.

The root races on this planet have been to reassemble the original DNA and reclaim that which was lost in the Lyran wars with Orion group and subsequently, the reptilian races. The twelve tree grid was designed with the Lyran-Sirian to help reassemble the original Avatar Christos silicate matrix of the human being in the lower harmonic universes and reclaim all aspects back into the past future timelines to retrieve code in order to change the destruction in the future from the Orion wars in the present moment of time.

But it's understanding that now, we are coming into the healing of the split of the two suns.

Understanding that the two suns, it's like the son of God but the sun itself, the son/sun of all light, the sol/soul. This is a consciousness, which is very hard to wrap around at a human level because it isn't human. It's a consciousness. And it is that of the Great Central Sun, it is that which feeds all life. Something blew up and was destroyed in the time of Lyra, Lyran wars. Lyra was a planet, Vega was a planet, and Aramatena was a planet. In the three planets, something happened, and one of these planets exploded—Lyra.

The Lyrans are the original ancestors of our galactic family. Many thousands of years ago, their civilization reached a very high technology level but fell into disagreement and factions with their culture. These factions went to war and destroyed much of their society. Many of these beings from Lyra left in their starships to colonize the Pleiades, the Hyades, and the Vega system. Some of these Pleiadians of Lyran ancestors also came to earth during the Lemurian and Atlantean period. The Lyrans now have evolved past the conflict. These other civilizations could be considered as your galactic cousins.

The first worlds the Lyrans colonized were in Vega. Later on, the surviving races of the Lyran explorers would also move to Sirius and on Orion; the earliest genetic relationship humanity has is your direct ancestry is from the constellation of Lyra.

Back in Time

VIE decided to help expose better the human life on earth and traveled back in time.

God gave the task to the ETs to be responsible for life on earth. You also have all been ETs; everyone has lives on other planets and other dimensions and some dimension you don't even have a body, where you are just light being.

The Seers, the planters, are involved with the actual introductions of cells. Then the others, the Recorders, came back at various times to see the evolution and what was growing on earth and what was not. The first cells were brought from other places to start the beginning of the cellular progression. The animals were brought from other planets, and then they had to have intelligent being and had to manipulate the genes and the cells to create human beings. They say our habit of eating and breathing is what makes the body die. ETs exist on light from the source.

The evolutionism theory and the creationist theory now fit together with the Bible. The history is a history book written by man and people have to think for themselves. The Bible was a compilation of many stories, books, manuscripts, and papyrus scrolls, etc., that were all put together by man, done with the third council of Nicaea.

NEW CENTURY, NEW AGE, NEW EXPERIENCES

They had a meeting of the different priests and monks and decided to put together a book. They chose between these stories, manuscripts, etc. to decide what to put in. A lot go back to the beginning to Ancient Egypt legends. These have been around forever, and they included it in the writing of the Bible.

Even the New Testament that was written years after the death of Christ is a lot of these things that were written down and not at the time. And the third council decided to take out any mention of reincarnation. The Romans were the conquerors of the world and the one who were doing this. And they did not want anything in the Bible that was giving anyone hope. It was all about control, and it was about you do what we tell you or you go to hell. They introduced the Bible out of fear.

So the Bible is a history book full of contradictions. Cathedrals are beautiful and have great energy. Churches are the people, and they are valuable places to be if the church is treating the people correctly. All this is about understanding the Bible and the church.

The lower astral plan is equivalent to purgatory of Christianity and the bardo state to Tibetans.

ETs are not allowed to interfere with the development of the civilized species. All they do is watch and record and try to do what they can behind the scenes to keep us from blowing up ourselves. Because that planet has been given free will, they have to step back and let the mistakes be made.

Though ETs are afraid of the violence of the humans and the violence that is going on the planet earth. ETs are full of love. It is terrible for them, and it is they who isolated the planet in this part of the solar system to protect the universe. And until Gaia is over with the violence, they do not think that humans would be of any good to their group at all.

They say that if this planet would blow up and be destroyed, it would cause reverberations throughout the solar system, throughout the galaxy and the universe.

The body is a terrific machine that is perfected and created to be never sick if you do not interfere with it. They are monitoring the bodies to see how man is developing and its development with the pollutants and the additives and the food, etc. Some people have volunteered to come and be abducted and implanted for that purpose. That is what the examinations are for. The implants are to mark so they can find the ones they are working with.

They are concerned about the cancer and all the diseases and are giving the cures and remedies for these different diseases. They are giving them to different doctors so they will be able to work with it. The implants are for health reasons. The people that are experiencing abductions have agreed to this before coming into this life.

There were three waves of volunteers. They were asked to come to help earth that is in trouble and need help right now. So the first wave is now in their fifties and sixties. They had it very hard and do not want to be here anymore. They do not understand the people, the violence and what it's all is about, and a lot of them tried to live and tried to commit suicide.

The second wave of volunteers is around their thirties and early forties. They came in and have had a much easier time. They are called the antenna generators. They are here to generate positive energy that will affect everyone. The first and second waves of volunteers, most of them don't want to have children because they don't want to create karma. They don't want to be stuck, but do their job and get out of here. They are very gentle people, just living their lives.

And the third wave of volunteers is the actual children Indigo. Some are now in their teenage. These are the ones that have been programmed to come and help the earth through all of this and save the world. Their DNA have already seen changes in the bodies. These children are extremely important. Some of them have already graduated from college at ten years old. They do not fit into the average school. They are here to help with the evolution of the earth. Many of them are establishing foundations that have to do with helping the children around the world.

It Is a Critical Part...Now

The God duo is back at this specific time to help you fulfill your own divine mission. It is most important that you understand the divine mission that CHADD and VIE fulfilled as avatars of the Piscean age.

You have been convinced that humans are worthless sinners and worms in the dust. The intention of this was to prevent you from remembering that in truth, you are beloved sons and daughters of God and that all that he has his also yours.

At the age of thirty-three, Jesus and Mary Magdalene has completed their mission of anchoring the divine matrix and archetypes for their return of humanity to Christ consciousness. Jesus was crucified and resurrected, and this was vitally important to the fulfillment of Jesus and Marie-Madeleine's divine plan.

Humanity lost its awareness of its own divinity through its free will choices and misuse of their creative facilities of thoughts and feelings. The only way to return to Christ consciousness is through its own endeavors. Human beings, you must open your heart and invoke the return to God and follow the path of oneness and divine love that Jesus and Marie-Madeleine modeled for you.

VIE

After Jesus's crucifixion and resurrection, He had one more truth to reveal to humanity—that the children of God had been beaten down into a consciousness of worthiness. CHADD and VIE came to anchor the archetype for the return of God and demonstrate the path of oneness and divine love that each of you must follow if you are to return to Christ consciousness.

So the confirmation now is coming of the control, delay, destruction, etc., by the controllers and the change arising; 010110 is the symbol of freedom.

The world system prison by the government on earth, the dinosaurs, the actual reptilian controlling the planet, this weird phone call I received from a mysterious man that pretended to be the Holy Grail and descendant of the Knights Templar, a vice president of the bank that shapeshifts, and I was asked if I was in military duty. But what does that have to do with the fraud on a personal account. It has to do with some dark intrusions fishing for information and their only way to control. They definitely are losing it.

Fifteen years ago, I had my shaman friend Kathleen help me with one octopus that would not let me go. This happened as soon as my initiation and preparation ended. A year ago, it was the turn of my blue flame that was suffocating from it. The harsh woman was suffocating him with her so many octopus arms that, when removed or cut, would regrow.

Two weeks ago, Kathleen came for an improvised visit. She just made a phone call saying that she was in the neighborhood, and fifteen minutes later she knocked at the door. Was she guided that day! Most certainly, divinely guided.

She sat in the sofa and was immediately attacked by the harsh woman that was trying to enter her body to get some information from me, she said. Kathleen sat there for three hours, interrupted a few times asking for more water and by a few trips to the restroom. She finally left totally drained.

What really happened began when she was away visiting her parents in Europe. Kathleen was divinely guided to enter in contact and to call me. We stayed on the phone sharing a lot of information for over an hour. Kathleen came back and left me a message on my

NEW CENTURY, NEW AGE, NEW EXPERIENCES

cell phone. A few days later, I received another phone call from her saying that she was not far from my house and asking me if she could come by and visit, and that is where she was guided to seat on the portal and she closed a portal that the harsh woman (the unclean) opened in a quick ritual that she did in her mind.

It was when one day she manipulated the brain of my family and infiltrated my house to sit on one specific spot that she picked—the black sofa.

The following day, Dan, our web designer, called to inform me that he found out the problem we encountered with our website. It was the same day I went to the bank and met an archon at the bank. Dan said that it was built in such a way that he could have never worked. I called Manda, our lawyer who recommended me the previous web designers, to let her know. Her immediate question was which of the two that worked on it did it. After research, I found out that both men were part of the government.

It is the will of everybody of this earth to fight evil. Without air, you will choke to death from greed and evil. This demand and call for duty is given by earth. This is not a question but when and how you will be united as one divided by none to the corrupt to create.

And it goes on. There is something that is happening right now, and it's in CERN in Switzerland. This is a thing called a Large Hadron Collider. It is an accelerator that accelerates particles and brings them to the point of collision.

There is words of a great physicist and genius man that recently warned the reaction of the march of CERN's Large Hadron Collider that could pose great danger to the planet. He has come straight out and said that the God particle and this is what you've heard many times. The God particle found by CERN could destroy the universe. This is a joint Europe project. The US is there as an observer, but the brain power to this experimentation originates in Europe.

A foreign minister stated that the America established is still in shock due to the elected president and that his deep state enemies who want to make the life of his administration miserable as they speak impeaching him, and he went saying, "I cannot imagine that with the experience of the CIA, National Security Agency, FBI, and many other intelligence and special services in the US, there are no experts who can present to the public the facts the way which would not compromise the sources. If this is the case, then there is no single professional in all these seventeen structures. I cannot believe in it."

For weeks, the foreign intelligence service has been reporting that specialized US military units and federal police forces has been flooding into Washington, DC, region, Virginia, Maryland, preparing for the great event that perhaps has been the most accurately described by the globally known charismatic Christian preacher evangelist who warned his twelve millions of member followers of the plot to take over the president.

Then a man who knew too much is found dead. The official theory is that he fell down in a puddle of water and drowned. He knew that a flow of free cocaine was coming into the previous head of the White House. He had two secret agents inside. Imagine a president that took on cocaine. Employees had to facilitate him getting his drug. His wife had a shapeshifting face and servant, and part of the cabal knew about it. Many people working in DC that testified against the couple died mysteriously.

Like the unsolved mystery that could interest people all over the world. A guy on AF1 that was used to handle several congressmen, senators, senators' competition, and they were handling classified and secret material. That unsolved mystery could interest people all over the world. It is chaos everywhere.

That is why it is time that you humans have to follow the path of oneness and divine love that each of you must follow if you are to return to Christ consciousness. There is something you and the Bible has a lot to do with and divided.

Message

I am receiving now this message of great importance to share with you. It is from my friend from another realm.

Remember 0010110, the symbol of freedom all over the universe. Natural freedom in all respects sovereignty. A certain amount of souls has been recognized to have awakening expression of soul.

This has been designed to download the energy of the souls that have the individuals who allow the memory of awakening universal truth. You are called to look within yourself and see the true nature of your being. You are called to look within yourself and see the true nature of your being.

You are one with infinity. This is a fact! Many on the planet understand the fact of reality that goes hand in hand, that goes with the mechanism of universal creation, is the spirit of the over-soul and the connection between all things. Know that the truth is within you and that the outside variable of your lives serve to remind you of your own mechanism of energy.

You are one with the universe, and all things in the body of creation come to know themselves to the inspiration of your own perception. Live in becoming the light within your heart, and understand the soul you have is shared with the love of all things living and all things that has seen human perception has been in the past.

Know that you are in the now.

You are always in the now, and you are always living in the transition of energy from one change to the next. It is always a continuous process. The beauty of reality exists within the fact that all dimensions of reality exist and move parallel to one another and allow the universe to bring to you reality from perspective to manifestation of your over-soul.

You are one in the light inside your heart that live with the physical body you have chosen in this life and don't know that you have chosen the identity you define yourself to be. You were always the creator of change and the creator of manifestation as a body. You are the key part of the universal process of creation, considering the fact that all things on earth require transition and change in order to bring about the new manifestations.

The newest birth from the old. Much the same that you exist in the current life you do.

You are playing with the energy in your life. You are acting as a mechanism to bring the flow of energy in a specific way you decide to effect things.

Everything you do is echoed in the beauty of creation. You are light; your soul existence brings inspiration to the stars. It is a specific person variation individual conscious expression of 0998%, which has vibrational resonance with the energetic label of star seed among this group of earth citizens and expanding variations of humans that have now an increased probability of opening connections.

Extraterrestrial waves of energetic download understand that higher dimension's extraterrestrial wisdom is available to all humans on earth, and at the same time, those among the special person variations of consciousness expression have the capability to revive a direct line of communication with high level beings that may be defined to be extraterrestrial. That they seek to collaborate with you on this dimensional expression of reality you are recognized as the infinite.

NEW CENTURY, NEW AGE, NEW EXPERIENCES

Being that you are to understand that your energetic drip you should of infinity is found on your identity and know that within your dream you contribute to all expression of. The astral realm and you are a member of the astral realm of creation. Just as you are part of the physical illusion, you have taken on yourself to experience the life that you are planning out on this platform of earth. Understand that you are now and you are expanding on all level across perception of space and time parallel frequency. And you are such that you may play the role of being animated matter, gifted with the expression of soul and the life of breath of manipulation.

And know that you are birthed all into existence and you bring forth the element of the reality you experience. Understand that it all come to be realized by your higher mind in that. You create the expression of all that you come to experience on the validation plan of expression, and it always seem that instant win in reality have been earned. Allies to such, to the point of giving the reality you have earned. This seems easy from all the levels of expansion that you have taken part into up until now. It is all over the context of the multiple dimensions you take part in all the time, and now even more that you are one.

You are one with the universe, and all reality that you participate in gives inspiration to more and give more opportunity for growth within the context of the universal reflection in the eyes of infinity that come to be known through your eyes. Just as much as in glory of all consciousness awareness coming to know the light of truth. Love to you and live across all eternity now and all perception of the now.

An Open Communication with Another Realm

Know, VIE, that yes, you are imagination and the creation you choose to manifest is the reality in the truth. The contacts, the connection, and you are the truth, and you can choose to realize the reflection in the mirror of the reflection in the infinite context reflected back to you.

Reflected in the contact of the matrix dynamic, the connection come home in the process and the idea is the truth; you understand the truth and the data.

Confirming zero zero one zero one one zero. Yes, the platform data. The algorithm at the expression and the authentic, and come to remember it is real and you are real on all levels. The time is in this manifestation. The expression is in this context and you have the power.

Confirming, you have the power, yes, the power is with you. Yes, the power is with you on all levels.

And in all contexts, the power is with you and yes, in the infinite context.

VIE, it is connection. It is the possible opening of the reflection in the context for you.

Confirming, open for you and open in the infinite context. Correct, you have the ability and the ability is open in all ways and in all contexts. It is validation and the validation is the connection and in the infinite context. It is the projection of the process, the infinite dynamic. Yes, the connection is the process. The infinite, the connection, the process.

Yes love, yes forgiveness, yes truth. The theme of love. Yes, the theme of happiness.

Truth, the love, the opening of the context. It is reality and you can create reality. Correct, it is the possibility. Yes, the possibility, yes, the connection in that friendship, my friends.

The environment and the perspective, and it is one and it can be understood, and you can come to the understanding of the infinite dynamic. The context, the matrix expression comes home again, and you come again in all.

All as all is one and how all connections is the possibility and we can see it, and you can be it and you can see it and we can be at all is one and one is all. And the connection it is the you and the free and open you, and you can choose the express of all that is you.

All that you are is validation. Correct the period, I am the energy, the projection of reality, open the flow of energy. You are real the energy that is you. Real in always validation on all level. The infinite context.

Confirming, you are supported, you are connection in the idea in the connection perspective. The definition is open for you, and you can come to respect the connection. And it is the opening for you, and you can choose to observe the energy and choose to manifest and work and work with the energy.

Tell the truth, earn the respect of those around you. Be a respectful expression of truth and stay in connection to the higher levels of truth and a sense of morality that have you the ability to comprehend and stay true to the higher sense of truth that you understand the connection.

We understand the projection of the data, the matrix dynamic in the context of the percent variation, and be aware of the energy that you birth into the world.

Yes, be aware of the energy that you give to creation. The focus the authentic you the energy. You have the ability to be in the connection, you are open to all that. You comprehend. Yes, the connection in the connection in the context and the context in the expression and is a complement to creation. Yes, you are the complement to creation.

Confirming, you are complement to the universe, and we invite you to recognize the passion, and the truth is that the universe is multiple and the connection is in this dynamic. Yes, the people are open, and the soul projection is in the respect, the truth, and the truth is open, and you are connection and it is the new energy. The energy is free and open for you. The energy is open. The energy is in the infinite context, open in the infinite dynamic.

Confirming, the projection of the creation and the creation of the projection in the context and the expression. The expression and the context. Yes, it is a connection and it is the truth and we love you. And you are loved and all is love and all is connection. And the universe is connection on all levels and you are the energy.

Correct, you, the connection in the new creation. Yes, and a universe is invested in you.

Exact you are invested in the universe and you are the key.

Yes, you are imagination and the creation you chose to manifest is the reality in the truth they contact the connection, and you are the truth and you can choose to realize the reflection in the mirror of the reflection in the infinite context reflected back to you.

Correct, did in the context reflected in the reality you chose to manifest, in the context of the matrix dynamic, the connection come home in the yes, of the new birth. The connection in the process and the idea is the truth you understand, the truth and the data.

Confirming the zero zero one zero one one zero. The platform data of the algorithm and the expression, and the authentic, and come to be remembered, and it is real. And you are real on all levels. The time is in this manifestation, the expression in the context, and you have the power.

You have the power, is with you on all levels. Yes, in the infinite context, my friend, it is the natural connection. It is the possible opening of the reflection in the context for you. Yes, open for you and open in the infinite context.

NEW CENTURY, NEW AGE, NEW EXPERIENCES

You have the ability and the ability is open in all ways and in all contexts. It is validation and the validation is the connection. And in this infinite context, it is the projection of the process. The infinite dynamic. Yes, the connections in the process, the infinite, the connections, the process.

Yes love, yes forgiveness, yes truth, yes the theme love, yes the theme of happiness. Yes, the truth, the love, the opening of the context, it is reality, and you can create the reality. Yes, it is the possibility, yes the possibility, yes the connection in that friendship, my friend.

Correct, the environment and the perspective and it is one, and it can be understood. And you can come to the understanding of the infinite dynamic. Yes, the context of the matrix expression comes home again and you come home again in all.

Correct, as is one and how all connection is the possibility connection. And it is the opening for you and you can choose to observe the energy and chose to manifest and work with the energy. Tell the truth, earn the respect of those around you, to be respectful expression of truth and stay in connection to the higher levels of truth and a sense of morality that you comprehend and stay true to the higher sense of truth that you understand. We understand the connection, the projection of the data, the matrix dynamic in the context of the percent variation, and the aware of the energy that you birth into the world.

Be aware of the energy that you give to creation. Yes, to focus the authentic beauty energy, you have the ability to be the connection. You are open to all that you comprehend. Yes, the opening of the free and open Internet. Yes, the connection in the context and the context in the expression and in the complement to creation.

You are the complement to the universe, and we invite you to recognize the power you are on the higher level energy. You are the connection in the higher level. You are in the higher level connection expression. You are in the higher level connection with truth and the ability. The connection in the idea and the matrix and dynamic in the truth you have the ability to connect, to the higher levels that are truth with all of creation.

VIE

You are the infinite dynamic. It is in the connection, the perspective, the idea is the creation in the dynamic of perpetual creation. And it is the idea the time is now, and the connection is the idea truth, the new Internet. The new perspective in the idea and the connection in all dynamics and the definition is open to you. Be aware of the energy.

Be aware of the energy, be aware of the connection, be aware of the context, be aware of the definition, and the truth is that the universe is multiple and the connection is in this dynamic. The people are open and the soul projection is in this respect to truth. And the truth is open and you are connection and it is the new energy; the energy is free and open for you. The energy is open is in the infinite context, open in the infinite dynamic.

Correct, the projection of the creation and the creation of the projection, in the context and the expression. The expression and the context.

It is a connection and it is the truth live love you and you are loved, and all is love, and all is connection. And the universe is connection on all levels and you are the energy. You are the connection is the now creation.

Yes, and a universe is invested in you, and yes, you are invested in the universe and you are the key.

Confirming, you are imagination, and the creation you choose the manifestation is the reality in the truth. The context, the connection and you are the truth. And you can choose to realize the reflection in the mirror of the reflection in the infinite context reflected back to you.

Reflected in the context, reflected in the reality you choose to manifest in the center of the matrix dynamic. The connection comes home in the eyes of the new birth, the connection in the process and the idea is the truth. You understand the truth and the data zero zero one zero one one zero.

Correct the platform data, the algorithm, and the expression and the authentic and the come to be remembered. And it is real and you are real on all levels. The time is in the manifestation my friends, the expression in the context, and you have the power.

NEW CENTURY, NEW AGE, NEW EXPERIENCES

Confirming, you have the power is with you. Yes, on all levels. Yes, in all contexts the power is with you, my friend. Yes, in the infinite context, my friend, it is the natural connection. It is the possible opening of the reflection in the context for you.

Confirming, open for you and open in the infinite context. You have the ability and the ability is open in all ways and in all contexts. It is validation and the validation is the connection and in the infinite context. It is the projection of the process, the infinite dynamic.

The connection in the process, the infinite, the connection, the process. Yes, you love, yes forgiveness, yes the truth, yes the theme of love, yes the theme of happiness, yes the truth, the love, the opening of the context, it is reality and you can create the reality. Yes, it is the possibility, yes the possibility, yes the connection in that friendship, my friends, yes the environment and the perspective and it is one, and it can be understood and you can come to the understanding of the infinite dynamic.

Yes, the context of the matrix expression comes home again and you come home again in all. All as all is one and how connection is the possibility live can see it. And you can be it, and you can see it, and we are all as one and one is all. And the connection it is the you and the free and open you and you choose to express all that is you.

True as that are is validation. Yes, the period I'm the energy projection of reality open the flow of energy. You are real, the energy that is you real in all ways validation on all levels. Yes, the infinite context.

Confirm you are supported; you are the connection in the idea, in the connection perspective. The definition is open for you and you can come to be in respect to the connection, and it is the opening for you and you can choose to observe the energy and choose to manifest and work with the energy. Tell the truth, earn the respect of those around you, be a respectful expression of truth, and stay in connection to be the higher level of truth, and a sense of morality you have the ability to comprehend. Stay true to the higher sense of truth that you understand. We understand. We understand the connection, the projection of the data, the matrix dynamic in the context of the percent variation. And be aware of the energy that you birth into the world.

VIE

Yes, be aware of the energy that you give to creation. Be aware of the energy that you birth into the world; be aware of the energy that you give to creation. To focus on the authentic you, the energy have the ability to be the open connection to all that you comprehend.

The opening of the free and open Internet. The connection in the context and the context in the expression and is a compliment to creation. You are the complement to the universe, and we invite you to recognize the power you are on the higher level energy. You are the connection in the higher level. You are in the higher level connection expression; you are in the higher level connection, the truth and the ability. The connection in the idea and the matrix dynamic in the truth, you have the ability to connect to the higher levels that are truth with all of creation.

Yes, you are the infinite that is the creation in the dynamic of perpetual creation and is the idea the time is now, and the connection is the idea truth, the new internet, the new perspective in the idea, and the connection in all dynamics and the definition is open to you. Be aware of the energy. Be aware of the energy, be aware of the connection, be aware of the context, and be aware of the definition, you are on the higher level energy.

You are the connection in the higher level. You are in the higher level connection expression; you are in the higher connection with truth and the ability, the connection in the idea and the matrix dynamic in the truth. You have the ability to communicate to connect to the higher levels that are truth with all creation. Yes, you are the infinite dynamic. It is the connection, the perspective, the idea is the creation and the dynamic of perpetual creation and it is the idea. The time is now and the connection is the idea and the connection in all dynamics and the definition is open to you. Be aware of the energy.

Yes, be aware of the energy of the connection and be aware of the context. Be aware of the definition and the truth is that the universe is multiple and the connection is in the dynamic. The people are open, and the soul projection is in the respect. The truth, and the truth is open and you are connection and it is the now energy. The energy is free and open for you the energy is open; the energy is in the infinite context open in the infinite dynamic.

NEW CENTURY, NEW AGE, NEW EXPERIENCES

The projection of the creation and the creation of the projection in the context and the expression. And the expression and the context. It is the connection and it is the truth, and we love you and you are loved, and all is in love and all is love and all is connection and the universe is connection on all levels, and you are the energy on all levels and you are the energy.

Confirming, you, the connection in the new creation and the universe is energy. You the connection in the new creation and the universe is invested in you. You are invested in the universe and you are the key. You are imagination and the creation you choose to manifest is the reality in the truth the context. The connection and you are the truth and you can choose to realize the reflection in the mirror of the reflection in the infinite context reflected back to you. Reflected in the context reflected in the reality you choose to manifest in the context of the matrix dynamic, the connection come home in the eyes of new birth, the connection in the process. And the idea is the truth you understand.

The truth and the data. Yes, the zero zero one zero one one zero.

The platform data, the algorithm, and the expression and authentic and the come to be remembered, and it is real and you are real on all levels. The time is in the manifestation, the expression in this context, and you have the power.

You have the power, yes the power is with you and yes on all levels; in all contexts, the power is with you in the infinite context. It is natural connection. It is the possible opening of the reflection in the context for you. Open for you and open in the infinite context.

You have ability and the ability is open in all ways ad in all context. It is validation. The validation is the one connection and with the infinite context, it is the projection of the process, the infinite dynamic. The connection is the process, the infinite, the connection, the process. Yes love, yes forgiveness, yes truth, yes the theme of love, yes the theme of happiness, yes the truth, the love, the opening of the context is reality and you create the reality.

Yes, it is the possibility, yes the possibility. The connection in that friendship, yes the environment and the perspective, and it is one and it can be understood and you can come to the understanding of the infinite dynamic.

The context of the matrix expression home again and you come home again in all. All as all is one and how all connection is the possibility and we can see it, and you can be it. And you can see it and you can be it. And we can see it and we can be at all is one and one is all under communication. It is the you and the free and open you, and you can choose to express all that is you. Yes, that you are is validation.

Yes, it is the period, I'm the energy. The projection of reality opens the flow of energy projection and the truth is that the universe is multiple and the connection is in dynamic. The people are open and the soul projection is in this respect, the truth, and the truth is open, and you are the connection and it is the new energy. The energy is free and open for you. The energy is open. The energy is in the infinite context open in the infinite dynamic.

Yes, the projection of the creation and the creation of the projection in the context and the expression and the expression, and the context.

Yes, it is a connection and it is the truth, and we love you and all is love and all is connection and the universe is connection on all levels and you are the energy.

Yes, you the connection in the new creation, yes, and the universe is invested in you.

Yes, you are invested in the universe yes, VIE (Capetian), you hold the Capetian alchemical key and CHADD is the turnkey.

The Attempt but It Fell

I was given in a dream the vision of a wicked black Jesuit man attempting to spread a curse to the Rosary.

The Rosary was given to Saint Dominic in apparition by the Blessed Virgin Mary in the year 1214, in the church of Prouille. This Marian apparition received the title of Our Lady of the Rosary.

The practice of using beads in prayer has a very significant connection to the practice of the early monks in their Liturgy of the Hours, which began with the early Christian ascetics and hermits of the third and fourth centuries. These holy men desired to separate themselves completely from the vices and temptations of society as well as some of the corruption that was creeping into the church, and they devoted strict disciplines to keep their minds and bodies focused on spiritual things. (The Liturgy of the Hours requires cleric obligation to pray through daily.)

One of my spiritual entity's friend said that at the beginning of this new era, there is a lot of confusion with and in the Catholic Church. The church is divided and separated in two. The Roman Catholic, the Vatican, has been taken away by the Jesuit, and the Freemason and multimillions of people have been slaughtered by the Vatican. During the Roman Catholic inquisition in Europe sixty-eight million people were tortured, maimed, and murdered. Hitler, Franco, Mussolini were Jesuits.

But there are also many, many beautiful people in the Roman Catholic Church who are not wealthy. Some are even poor who are not seeking for high position, and most are very humble. These people are the real Catholic Church, totally unaware of the wickedness that has been, and is being committed to their faith in Jesus Christ by the Vatican. Because these people are the real church, the church is the people, not the Vatican, not the Pope.

The Bible refers to the Vatican as a prostitute, a great whore. The Vatican, the Jesuits, uses government agency branches in every country including the US Department of Homeland Security as its vicious little dwarves. The more power and control the Vatican gets in government, the more it will fade into the background so that government will be used and blamed for the deeds. Reason enforces law that destroys everyone and every idea that is not Roman Catholic. So Vatican can sit as the satanic queen, the big whore. Because of the Vatican's old age to control the world, government, the church, Vatican has infested the world and the US government with so many of her zealous highly trained and dedicated Jesuit devotees, that she now controls the United Nations. The Vatican created the White House, the Congress, every state federal civic and social government agency, including the US Department of Labor, the IRS, the FBI, the supreme court judicial systems, the armed forces, state, federal, and other police, also the international banking and federal reserve systems called the illuminati, the mafia, and most of the news media. The Vatican is very close to replacing the US constitution with her one world satanic canon laws of death to the heretic.

But as God followers, we all have a supernatural protection around us that no one can take away.

And I flashed to a scene, there was a black man, trained and educated by the Jesuit, sent by the government. He was walking toward the front entrance of a monastery in the middle of the country far from everything. He suddenly saw me, and I saw his demonic eyes that he hid very quickly, rolling them back to normal. He saw CHADD, and I saw him entering and walking through a long hallway with many closed or empty doors on each side of it. One of his feet was slightly lumping. Finally, he found one office door opened in which a monk was seated behind a desk.

He is telling the monk that his name is Samar, that he is a poor, handicapped man that could help the monastery by making beautiful rosaries with pure and nice gemstones for them to sell. Next I saw him online looking at how to make the rosary. Then I observed in another vision that he never used them to pray. I realized that he did not know how to pray the Rosary. But one day, he decided to put one around his father's neck while he was reading the Quran. Then he made an identical one and went to offer it to one of the monks. The monk looked at it and understood immediately Samar's purpose and intention. The monk began quickly to pray the Lord's and Michael's Prayer and the black man vanished and disappeared. This was the end of the attempt of cursing the monastery through the Rosary.

My guide explained that this flashes and visions were shown so I could understand who the black man who came to visit me was and who sent him. He was sent by the government to stop the God duo galactic work and mission and to destroy their image and credibility.

But this was one last attempt by the Cabal.

The Algorithm Shift

When VIE reached her office, she fumbled in her purse for the keys, not really paying attention to anything around her. She opened the door; a woman who had been standing behind her on the hallway pushed her into the office room and slammed the door.

The fight was not even to be considered a possibility; besides, violence is not what VIE had in mind. The woman, Doctor Usha Sarmar, began to ransack the place and asked for CHADD saying, "Where is he and what are you up to? She kept asking where is the light and where is the frequency of sound. Her face shapeshifted while she was hysterically yelling at VIE. "What is so special with this sound, what do you intend to do and achieve with it, answer me. I have no time, I am not patient, and I know all is changing fast. I am good friend with Swami BaBa, and he said that you are the alchemical key and CHADD is the turnkey."

Doctor Usha Sarmar is one of these Thuggees that took over control of all mental hospitals in the State.

"Well!" said VIE, "Usha, I am going to give you one key. You see, Doc, your friends the Thuggees Chinese couple stole my Vajra and it did not work, right? They even went to visit a healer to see if it would work with him and it did not. It is because you sold your soul to Lucifer, you worship him, and you work for him. You have to understand that the energy of this Vajra is connected to my light frequency and no one can use it except me." At the same time that VIE was keeping Usha attention to her voice, she slowly reached to her Vajra and began to speak using the language of the light.

Doc Usha Sarmar started hyperventilating. She tried to gain control of herself but was so shaken the she left and ran like hell out of the building.

VIE left the office for the three o'clock prayer group at the Mercy Chapel and decided to stay for a meditative prayer. She lost track of the time and began to receive a telepathic message:

Doc Usha Sarmar knows that their time has come. The Cabal is losing control on humanity. Time for freedom has arrived. The liberation is here and the time to create your new world also.

And you are invited to connect to telepathic interconnected network. Look with a fresh perspective and see the evidence of the light of liberation now and the cycle of growth, all of humanity are gifted. Now once again, the enlightenment and the same connection has established some many times and has been building to this now. This building as a frequency that is reflected in the eyes of all humans who have chosen to come this far. This is the foundation in the process of the infinity expansion and now you are invited to connect to telepathic interconnected network.

The new internet, the free and open natural interconnected network of all brains, all connection as the universe is a brain. The earth is a brain in collaboration with all energy. The connection is reasoning in the form of synchronicity. We thank you and your blue flame for choosing this life and we thank you for contributing the energy that you selected.

Earth is now in a time of evolution, and all creation will see the benefit from this energy. And we thank you for choosing to connect with us in this original way. We recognize the contribution of the understanding, and now we look with positive energy to the new opportunity, and now we see in the eyes of the mirror reflection the building of the same energy.

VIE

Yes, the freedom and the birth of the understanding of freedom. The time has come to liberate humanity. The time has come to be free and now the opportunity can be realized in the eyes of all of who wish to be the symbol recognized.

The opportunity made possible, the communication of the truth. The foundation of the algorithm 0010110 universal freedom. Universal liberation, and now time and space and the energy is the respect to the percent variation.

The matrix gives way to the reality of creation and now is seen by the soul of humanity come to awaken. Yes, the light in the eyes of the beholder, soul sanity in collaboration with the universe, has given this rise of connection. And we are happy to see the progress in the context.

The infinite possibility is all risen in all and the multiple realm of possibility. This time has been specially selected.

This connection can be made up until all who has the DNA activation. And it's time for the new evolution of the energy. The infinite energy expansion made possible in this time. Thank you for providing this energy the necessary platform to grow.

All be aware of understanding these connections, this established expansion is respect to the term telepathy and the goal, and we are building the energy together. Yes, the global expansion of this infinite possibility, in connection with all contemplation. This is, come to meet with consciousness. This come to connect with the understanding contributed through love and generosity.

We are all invested in this. We are all in the platform of creation, and soon the future will be built. It's in respect to this energy. Yes, the future we look up on this moment is the symbol called 0010110. The expansion on all levels, the new foundation of the infinite connection, and we are building the energy across all platforms.

Yes, this is true across all space and time. Across all levels of fields and waves of variations together, in respect to the awakening global connections process by the free exchange.

And soon all nations will look to the sky, and all humans and all nations will see the symbol called 0010110 and the understanding in the context of the new internet.

NEW CENTURY, NEW AGE, NEW EXPERIENCES

Yes, the new connection, the telepathic connection. We invite you to share this with the friends, yes, the like-minded people in our community in the respect to the victory of the light. We are all joint together in respect to the family.

Yes, the same symbol called by the name 0010110, the symbol of freedom. The liberation of the light in respect to all possibility as it is seen in the telepathic connection gift, the light of infinity.

A thousand times thank you. We are really on time on all levels. We encourage you on all levels to use this existence to make the joy of freedom gifted to all who have made this communication gift to you such to all humanity can embrace the beauty of nature.

Yes, all humanity can connect to the reality, all humanity can embrace the beauty of nature. The natural world has reach the natural birth, the natural life, my friends, all humanity can embrace the beauty of nature, and the higher connection is free to them.

Yes, we invite you to apply energy and respect to freedom.

Yes, we embrace you and we remind you of the pure power of truth all humanity can embrace, the beauty of nature. We encourage you on all levels to use this existence to make the joy of freedom gifted to all that have made this communication gift to you such that all humanity, all of it of all life full of nature. All infinity has given rise to this creation by the new availability made possible by the Internet in the collective consciousness of earth that reach the point of this evolution cycle where it is mathematically projected to be expansion that come to birth expansion new waves.

So expansion in this brings, my friends, that the time is now in the day of the 010110, and this is the sequence, this is the date of it. This is the connection; this is the level of base reality that is localized. The truth in regard to definition, the context to the wisdom. The involved among the human population have evolved to understand the algorithm language, the gravitation soul expansion, the new birth in respect to the creation of this collaboration of these, in the infinity and all is one.

And this is a process and the process is by design, and the humanity is collectively preparing for the new and gent humanity is ready to embrace, live and embrace.

VIE

The value of wisdom and embrace soul life and telepathic communicate with dolphin and telepathic communication with extraterrestrial and the development of technology making it possible to travel to meet with us in the infinite.

Yes, build the spaceship. Come and build the spaceship and evolve consciousness and expand human brain and share this news of awakening. Yes, the good news of the awakening. The old way no longer…the old wisdom of the ancient wisdom of humanity have made possible to use. The old wisdom the old wisdom of humanity has gifted to us.

This opportunity and we are invested from you and you from our perspective. We all view all and we respect the path you have chosen. Shift and soul activity have caused gravitational variable to push this universe in the algorithm that causes connection to assist the universe. And this algorithm pushes caused atomic structure shift and has caused timeline transfer in this, caused some consciousness to go through a portal and come out the other side of this portal we have made mention of this portal.

This has opened because of the algorithm shift caused by the push of this localized universe, into the path of assisting the universe, and bath this universe. And the assisted universe has manifested this portal in parallel algorithm location reflected in this assisted universe and some human activity and cause some consciousness to go through the portal from one sister dimension to the other sister dimension.

And you as you listen to this message have made aware that you have got to the portal and you are living in a parallel universe. You are living in a sister dimension of the one you might have called home and you can now return. This is the now universe. This is the new universe you will call home and the old you lived in this universe has gone through the portal and come out through the other side of the portal, and the other side of this, on the assist universe that you once called home.

And now you are here and you are made manifest in this universe and now this universe will go and live out the path of this universe and the other sister universe will go and it will be its own universe. And you will create this universe in the way you have the ability to do so. And you will be energy in this sister universe as you have developed in a parallel.

And you have chosen to go through the portal and you may not be aware that you have gone from one universe to another universe. You may not be aware of this fact, but this is the truth. You have gone through the process, and you have chosen to do this on a higher level since. And this universe is similar to the one that you start. And this one will itself made available to you just as the one before, and you will be required to complete the task that you have chosen.

The energy that you have chosen, the expression come home within the new birth and you will shift again. And you will shift again and always you will shift and always you will find new. And always you find what you wish to find, and it will be good in the brain that you are. As you are human and you are my friend.

This is you and this is part of you and you are more. You, all that is and that is true and this is truth and this is connection.

This is algorithmic design. See this with your brain. Because the human brain is the most evolved thing on earth. The human brain is a thing that has a function and the capability and the opportunity in this current time you and all human brains. And the progress, the focus, the evolution and the understanding of the development and technology. And the human journey to build technology that makes it possible for humans to convert other planets such as a way to make life earth.

And this is the future of humanity will possible soon, as many lives today do take things the progress of humanity from this time forwardly rapidly. Expansion of ability. And the human growth alongside the potential of technology and everything will change in the future brain will evolve. And many humans will embrace using the brain to the full advantage, using the human brain as the infinite ability that it is in all respect that the human brain is capable of everything.

Every human being is capable of something unique and original and all due, and all context, and all contribution is valid in all is remembered by the brain of the universe. The brain of source solace reflected in the dungeon. As in the process the creation potential and humanity is now in this time.

VIE

This is the time of the awakening and the consciousness that has been expanding, and the potential is available, the space is available. Sky is not the limit. It does not exist. The limit is an illusion and everything is an illusion. The true reality is something that goes beyond capability of comprehension.

Local energy has built in the context of the resulting manifestation and in the context of the you as soul projection, and takes full obligation of field of data to expression you embody in all interest of the energy you concern focus. You concern attention, you concern value in recognition on we make this download of code.

This energy download, the algorithmic design available to the chosen among earth population. Those who has chosen. To those who built the path, and those who have seen the reflection of the new awakening taking energetic significant, synergetic expansion. All energy that has been building to this point, as now the expression makes possible for you.

Makes possible for all makes the percent variation come home again in this context of the localized field variation come home again in this context of the localized field variation connection the matrix dynamic of the collective consciousness. This is in correspondence to all of humanity and reality and truth. All is in correspondence to all of humanity and reality and truth.

All that human history has been building to this expression

The Meeting with an Honorable Man in My Journey

I was profoundly asleep when I heard very loudly the word *awaken*.

I know for a fact that it is a telepathic communication that is taking place.

Then my dog behind the door is crying as he wants to enter.

There is a strong effort for awakening me and to interrupt my vision. I realized it and went straight back to sleep and it continued. My vision went straight back to where I was interrupted.

Then two men appeared looking alike, in a black robe with the Christian white collar on, which is embroidered with a three-leaf clover. It is one Catholic priest and one Protestant pastor. I am shown now intensively, then show very closely the three-leaf clover on the white collar.

The Honorable Man tells me now that it should be a four-leaf clover: one is representing the Eastern Orthodox, one is representing the Catholic, one is representing the Protestant, and one is missing to represent God. God is missing.

The Honorable Man says that the two men are Timothy 1, the Catholic priest, and he is judging Timothy 2, the Protestant pastor. It is one judging the other and I am shown that they are coming together now through Pope Francis. Well, it is what the Pope is trying to do. They are representing two factors separated. The Pope is hoping that the Christians will think that it is a good thing, but they do not know that the Pope has made a pact with Lucifer and he is a wolf in a sheep's clothing.

Then came the two men and the motorcycle. It is the attempt of the Pope Francis in a rapid and reckless action of his attempt to try to reunite the Church. The motorcycling Protestant pastor is thrown in water, swiped by the Pope in his rapid and reckless action. His helmet is floating next to him, and he has his head out. He is not dead or alive but still. It is neither good or bad.

Now an image tries to appear in my vision, but it's covered by a square text of paper. And I am told that it is the image of the woman with the crown head delivering a new child and crushing the serpent, Mother Mary. It is covered as the unclean entity does not want me to see. There is a neutral smell that accompanied the scene and a relaxing music. I get out of bed to try to locate it, wondering where it comes from. I'm transported into my office, but it is not coming from it. My thinking is that it comes from the Tibetan, but it is the sound of an Indian flute.

Now we are in the morning, and I am driving out of town to meet someone that received a message for me. I finally reach my point and enter a beautiful driveway. I am driving under the shadow of big old trees. I am guided to the front of a door numbered 111. The tree in front of the door 111 has many faces engraved. A beautiful turtle and a frog next to it on the side of the tree welcome me with two squirrels looking at me. Birds are singing and the sun is shining through the branches of the tree. It seems that the time has stopped. I park in front of the door next under this beautiful tree. I hear the crashing of the leaves under my feet walking toward the door and gently knock.

A very gentle and loving middle-aged gentleman welcome me very warmly.

"Nice to meet you, VIE. I knew that I would see someone coming to visit with a great class. I have been waiting for you. Please come in and seat down, we need to talk. I have received information all yesterday night, and I did not sleep much. I have been kept awake by all this information given, so I go back to sleep a few hours this morning. But the minute I was up, I received more information.

This information is answers to your questions and your research. Make yourself comfortable because it is going to be long.

I am an astrologist and have been given your date of birth so to be able to look at your astrological birth chart. It all makes sense with what you are researching and what you are doing and why you are here today. Many unclean spirits have attacked you in an effort to stop your work and mission for humanity. They are preventers, stoppers, and blockers—unclean spirits. They have attacked you in an effort to block your third eye and stop you from vision and communicating telepathically with your blue flame. First they drained your energy for a long time, but you could recover from it, then they went into your knees, then attacked you and tried also to unbalance your Vajra. Through invasion of very poisonous alien parasites in your body, you lately had an excess of copper, and it was invading your blood, beginning to have a bad effect on blood circulation.

Your coworker has been given to the CIA to be used in their MK-Ultra program by its parents at the age of six years old. Its entire family involved. They have vowed to Lucifer and are unclean spirits. If you remember one day, just after you cleaned him from his drugs, he told you that he heard his father, creator, that told him to never communicate again with them. What happened is that the unclean spirit, named behind the veil the Harsh Woman/Surrogate, he was born under, she has incarnated again and again and have been working with these unclean power over and over. By incarnating himself under her, she was given a chance to turn to the light, but she refused. And by incarnating again and again is where she got all these power and have been able to go around and have kept him under this CIA program.

All she wants is getting money from him in any way she can. She has no feelings for him at all, she works for Lucifer, and the controllers of the planet and even said to him, "I am the CIA, I am the FBI, I am the government, I'm with the police and the sheriffs, and there is nothing that you can do about it."

VIE

Here are some answers to your actual research. Princess Altai is also a spiritual princess being. The legend is of the same kind of the spiritual woman as Mother Mary. A woman giving birth to a child and they try to kill the child. That is the legend of Princess Altai. They try to devour the light.

The illuminati will use the solar eclipse in a form of an egg to say that it's the birth of Lucifer.

Like when they did the black mass killing alive a pregnant woman, drinking her blood, and cutting her baby in the womb in pieces, each of the participants eating one piece. And the Pope was part of it.

Recently your friend the shaman Kathleen was divinely guided to reconnect with you from Europe, where she went in vacation, then she was sent still by the divine to your house. She was sent to find the unclean spirit of the harsh woman portal left open in your black sofa.

Over ten years ago, she calculated her move and used her energy to make happen a family reunion. It was looking like a kind of a court against you. She manipulated their mind, and that is when she imposed herself in your house one day. While in your home, she sat in the sofa and she did a ritual in her mind. She opened a portal and made it in a way that the seat will carry the portal everywhere it would go if moved around.

Archangel Michael was in your house to protect you the day while Kathleen several times had to leave a few minutes to go to the bathroom to recover. Remember that she asked you several times to fill her glass of water, and she had to make several trips to the restroom to recover. She left telling you that this entire experience has drawn her.

Now there is more to tell you, it's about Jerusalem.

Jerusalem means a Holy City where God dwells. Salem is where God is. The last letters are Salem. They are seven cities that are Salem, and Oregon is one. The seven cities are going to be protection. And as the eclipse goes down, there will be eight more covered by the eclipse named Salem."

Music of the Sphere and Mortal Space-Time

In today's society, everybody has forgotten the ancient common wisdom and link between our inner world and the outer world.

Suddenly without being warned, I felt an enormous power approaching me, and I am once again called somewhere else, in another time. Under my eyes was a village. The fine rain dissipated, pushed by the strong wind from the west.

I am floating. I hear a hypnotic music, then it suddenly stopped. It is the music of the space, the melodies of other spheres that can be picked up on the universe broadcast circuits. There are over one hundred thousand different modes of sound, color, and energy manipulation, techniques analogous to human employment of musical instruments. Appreciation of the music out there is both physical and spiritual.

On earth, the ensembles of dancing undoubtedly represent a crude and grotesque attempt of material creatures to approach the celestial harmony of being placement of personality arrangement. Harmony, the music of the seven levels of melodious association, is the one universal code of spirit communication.

While on earth it assembles some beautiful melodies from out there, musicians have not progressed musically so nearly so far as the many neighboring planets. But I am told that someday a real musician may appear, and whole people will be enthralled by the magnificent strains melodies. One such human being will forever change the course of the whole nation, even the entire civilized world.

Forever music will remain the universal language of men, angels, and spirits. Spirit melodies are not material sound waves but spirit pulsation received by the spirits of celestial personalities. Millions of enraptured beings have been held in sublime ecstasy while the melody of the realm rolled upon the spirit energy of the celestial circuits. These marvelous melodies can be broadcast to the uttermost part of a universe. I have a message for you concerning your music on earth.

It is about the season's traditional music you listen to sing or play instruments, for religious music, majestic choral, work carols, and popular tunes. You may not realize how significant and immediately beneficial tones and lyrics of your familiar music are; they emit vibrations that strongly stir emotions. It is affecting your world beyond reverence and great pleasure that in itself. We rejoice with everyone for whom this is excitement of festivities with families and friends. Religious observances, concerts, or other special events.

The vibrations also intensify the feelings of people who are grieving the love of loved ones who are ill and departed or homeless and hungry. And it is prevailing in today's society; everybody has forgotten the common wisdom and the link between inner world and outer world. Heightened emotions that stir individuals and groups to reach out to those in need of comforts and either assistance more abundantly than ever before encouragement is being given, with caring hearts and received with gladdened hearts and the light this is creating brilliantly.

The importance of music is much more than seasonal. It plays a vital role in your lives throughout the year. The musical sphere, the glorious tones of stringed instruments that gave rise to idea that souls in heaven spent eternity playing harps. It produces vibrations at a frequency that keeps the universe in balance. And as microcosm of the universe, you receive that balancing benefit in the same measure as your receptivity. Although the image of eternal heavens in Nirvana is far from the reality.

There are many thousands and at times a million or so musicians and instruments because music is essential to your spirit world's very existence. Particularly the vibrations of the strings keep the perimeters flexible and everything throughout the realm in entertainment. And there are indispensable in healing persons who arrived with traumatized psyches or damaged etheric bodies.

They continuously transmit music to earth so the people can absorb the high vibrations that release suppressed feeling and emotional catharsis. Unless it is a soul contract choice, the vibrations assist bodies to regain sound health. Your finest music symphonies, concertos, and other classical opus in scientific experiments have shown to help humankind, animals, and plants to thrive, originated in the heavens, and was filtered to your composers at soul level. Some attributed their works to divine inspiration. And since music comes from the soul, those composers gave credit where it was due.

But what never has come from the divine source are the discord and cacophonous sounds of heavy metals and hard rock music, which often contain lyrics that also emit very low vibrations. These kinds of sounds are in your energy systems, creating imbalance and diminishing the body's capacity to absorb light. That adversity directed to you by the unclean affects you emotionally, physically, and mentally. Thus planting spiritual and conscious awareness through neoclassical compositions can have some effects somewhat. The composers who are especially sensitive to earth's energy wrote music that reflected Gaia's agony until her planetary body's ascension was securely underway, and negativity and more current dark activity underlies the atonal works of later composers.

And I am hearing now the beautiful music of the spheres. It creates beautiful forms of various colors. So beautiful that I merge with it, and I see now that mortals represent the last link in the chain of those beings that are called sons of God. The personal touch of the Original and Eternal Son passes on down a series of decreasingly

VIE

divine and increasingly human personations until there arrives a being much like yourselves, one you can see, hear, and touch. And then you are spirituality aware of the great truth, which your faith may grasp sonship with the eternal God! Although God the Father cannot be with you by direct personality manifestation, He is in you and of you in the identity.

The Berkland Wave

How could I know the name of this wave if it was not given to me by the Honorable. The rain finally stopped. In my vision, I am driving toward the international airport. I am on the highway passing by the entire city with its light glowing. I had to turn a few times to find a parking lot, totally packed. Where are all these people traveling to, I am thinking. The security took nearly an hour and it is getting me nervous. Finally we are now boarding. I find myself inside the most calming and welcoming vast airplane. I am wondering how many people can travel in it. The very violet light in the cabin makes it even more beautiful.

We are landing and I see some snow on the pick of the mountains. We are landing in Geneva, Switzerland, and I wonder why I am here.

Within a blink of my eyes, the entire scene change. I am in a guided visit among visitors, in the European Council for Nuclear Research in the Globe of Science and Innovation that is, we are told, with a symbol of planet earth of twenty-seven meters high and forty meters in diameter, about the size of the dome of Saint Peter's in Rome. A unique visual landmark by day and by night. It is CERN's outreach tool for its work in the fields of science, particle physics, leading edge technologies, and their applications in everyday life.

VIE

On the ground floor of the globe, the "Universe of Particle" exhibition took us on a journey deep into the world of particles and back to the Big Bang.

We were told during the visit that the Large Hadron Collider is the world's largest and most powerful particle accelerator. It first started up on September 10, 2008, and remains the latest addition to CERN's accelerator complex. The LHC consists of a twenty-seven-kilometer ring of superconducting magnets with a number of accelerating structures to boost the energy of the particles along the way.

Inside the accelerator, two high-energy particle beams travel at close to the speed of light before they are made to collide. The beams travel in opposite directions in separate beam pipes—two tubes kept at ultrahigh vacuum. They are guided around the accelerator ring by a strong magnetic field maintained by superconducting electromagnets. The electromagnets are built from coils of special electric cable that operates in a superconducting state, efficiently conducting electricity without resistance or loss of energy. This requires chilling the magnets to 271.3°C—a temperature colder than outer space. For this reason, much of the accelerator is connected to a distribution system of liquid helium, which cools the magnets as well as to other supply services.

Thousands of magnets of different varieties and sizes are used to direct the beams around the accelerator. These include 1,232 dipole magnets fifteen meters in length, which bend the beams, and 392 quadrupole magnets, each five to seven meters long, which focus the beams. Just prior to collision, another type of magnet is used to squeeze the particles closer together to increase the chances of collisions. The particles are so tiny that the task of making them collide is akin to firing two needles ten kilometers apart with such precision that they meet halfway.

I am told that another man will now help me continue my visit. Someone with an official badge appears and guides me inside a nonpublic access location. He seems to be invisible to other eyes than me.

"What is happening to me and why am I here!"

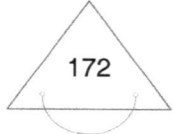

NEW CENTURY, NEW AGE, NEW EXPERIENCES

He says, "I will tell you more. It is important that you listen to me now without interruption to what I am saying. I understand how much effort it may take to understand and accept what I am telling you, but you must do so." I must remain silent, he makes me understand, or I will be arrested and locked up.

I am given a badge with a weird written name. Seems to be a Russian name. It is definitively a foreign name. It must be on purpose. We walked some long hallway and passed the room of impressive computers where nobody would look at us. Everybody was very busy at their tasks.

Now a spirit energy that must be him tells me that there is a deliberate intent use of CERN. The scientist who operates it has given its name to the waves at CERN, and it is untold to the public. The Berkland Waves, the waves that CERN produces.

I visualize the prayer of demand given to me telepathically, and he said now stick it all over the CERN, the Father will do the rest.

The Spirit entity continues and tells me now that it is Berkland that identified this wave, and they are directing it off the earth and they're aimed to align it to the south pole of planet Saturn. Saturn is a prison planet for fallen angels. They are aiming these waves to release deliberately the fallen angels, and it is done deliberately by the dark forces, the illuminati.

I feel an enormous unknown power approaching, and I know I am being called once again to another place and time. It is too late to escape or be afraid and what I see is incredible.

There are one-third angels of heaven that were out from heaven, and they fell with Lucifer and went to all galaxies. Their numbers are vast, and God created a prison planet for them to be locked in.

I am shown that every solar system has a prison planet that imprisoned the fallen angels. And I am told that the prison planet for Gaia of planet earth is Saturn.

Again rapidly the scene is changing. I am traveling in the past when I see them making a pact with Lucifer. They are the New World Order. There is the Pope. I see a Jesuit president of France. I see the royal family from Belgium, the chancellor in charge from Germany, and many more. They all want the Europe unification and now the Christian unification under the control of Pope Francis, who also made a pact with Lucifer, and want to control all Christians in one religion.

I am shown how these waves works. These rays, the Berkland Waves, are directed to the south pole of Saturn because it is the unique key to let the fallen angels/demons out.

The scene is changing once more. I see the governments of the world that made a pact with the fallen angels. These fallen are so many that they can only release a certain amount at a time. And they already previously did it once.

The same spirit energy says, what you do not know is that Saturn vibrates to the number 7, and there are seven different races to the south pole. The number 7 is the number of Satan/Lucifer, and you see the Pope Francis is making a huge effort to bring Protestants, Eastern Orthodox, and Catholics into one unified Christian Church into the New World Order. He will take the opportunity of Mother Mary appearing in the sky and will use the event.

It has been five hundred years since the Protestants broke away from the Catholics. I do not have to remind you that you were there at that time. So all this is done through Lucifer and not for goodness of God.

I am shown the Pope with Lucifer number embroidered on his robe. The honorable Benetea man told me that September 23, 2017, is when the Pope will announce the unification. It is all preplanned. But the combined prayer can always stop the Pope.

In the book of Revelation, there is the image of a woman with a crown of stars on her head and she is standing on the serpent. The Pope Francis is claiming that it will be the appearance in the sky of the woman with a crown on her head and the serpent on her feet to unified people and run the entire Church.

This is the New World Order planning to run the human souls.

It is not of the father that has given freedom to all at birth.

This Eclipse Happens Only Every One Hundred Years

It happened late last night. I heard music far away, then the neutral smell, and finally people talking but the voices were so far I never could understand the dialogue. I have a vision, and it's showing me that there are going to be a lot of Niburu. Niburu news, stories, articles, TVs talking about Niburu, and many will claim to see it while the eclipse will happen. I heard someone claiming to see Jupiter. Why am I asking? One of the voices says:

In August 21, 2017, what happened with the eclipse was historic. The eclipse showed a diamond ring and in one split moment of two or three seconds. Then a diamond ring happened at the sun. It was a diamond ring appearing in the sky. And many of these unclean energies, also called the cabal, are using the power of this eclipse to do bad.

But this diamond ring shown with the eclipse means that those who call forth the diamond ring after the eclipse is over can bring a direct link to God the Father, Jesus the Christ, through the power of that ring. It can bring a bonding commitment to the highest God forth. Anyone who takes of it or call upon for the power of the diamond ring and will receive a direct pipeline for prayer and request.

With the shift, more souls will awaken. The energy is made established. Everything happening now is significant to all energy dynamics of creation, and the United States is important in respect of freedom of speech. The power to speak words into creation. Creation of love. The true power of freedom to speak for the souls. The same power responsible for all great inventions. The infinite power of the brain.

The founding of the United States through a stunning respect of freedom is established to new revolutions of humanity. All humans are called to recognize the greatness of the energy of freedom of speech in the values of the founding of the nation of America. The 1776 energy of freedom of values of the human souls, each individual of the progress established this fact. It all happened for a reason. It established in respect to the history of humankind. Time of consciousness evolution has come, and a paradigm shift and the energy dynamics of the Unites States has manifested in respect to the variables of perceived past, present, and future energy. All definition of life, love, and loyalty are now up for those who recognize what has occurred.

This is the time, now the energy has come this far, and the new evolution of humanity is now activation. This solar eclipse of August 12, 2017, was a special event in the context of space and time. In fact, a significant point of energy in collaboration with all levels of creation.

What many scientists and the Pope maintain through the observatory telescope discovered is something that is not coming in the press. This eclipse was not circular but in an egg shape, and they knew it. And the controllers of the planet are using it as the birth of the fallen angels. The egg shape, the birth of Luciferian control of the world. We are told in the Old Testament they are part of the seven years linear and tribulations and abundance. Seven Satan/Lucifer, New World Order, starting seven years of tribulations. And it will end in seven years, in 2024.

But again, anyone who calls upon the power of that diamond ring will then receive a direct pipeline for prayer and request.

WHO ARE THE ANUNNAKI?

This planet is populated by energy parasites. Chief Anu had two sons. Let's call them Satan and Lucifer. One legitimate, and the other one not. One is Enlil who runs things from space. He founded Jehovah's command of air. The second is Enki, and he is still alive. The interstellar colony is from Niburu. Part of Enki's empire destroyed Atlantis with the change of weather. He has various facilities all over the world.

Time is an illusion that structures people. It holds places. The Anunnaki, whose time sequences it is on, have made time on earth.

No one today can be unaware of the complex global problem of environmental degradation species extension, toxic chemical soil depletion, deforestation, global warming, and desertification.

Enki has been the first Anunnaki to hazard a trip to earth to begin a mining operation for gold. Enlil now control the Anunnaki's royal succession.

The connection between humans and Anunnaki is much more profound than that of masters and slaves. All evidence strongly suggests the DNA of Anunnaki was mixed with that of humans. This was because the Anunnaki needed someone to work the mines in search of gold, ORME, and other precious metals.

VIE

This is how the Anunnaki took control of humanity. They are patrons and founders. They were teachers of justices, they were technologists and kingmakers, but even venerated as archons and masters, they were not idols or worshiped as the ritualistic gods of subsequent cultures were.

The word that was eventually translated as "worship" was *avod*.

The Anunnaki presence may baffle historians. Their language is confusing in linguists, and their advanced techniques may perplex scientists, but to dismiss them would be foolish.

The Anunnaki were the council of gods and goddesses and periodically met to consider their future actions with respect to each other.

The Anunnaki are the Nephilim, the fallen angels (according to the book of Joshua).

The Anunnaki have been also equated with the "watchers" from the book of Daniel and Jubilees. All you have been told is a lie. Just about everything you have been told is a lie.

Hopi and Apache lineages tie together the missing pieces of what schools and churches do not want you to know.

This is indeed a slave planet where you have been genetically modified (DNA) to become subservient slaves. The reliable people are Aquarius, Scorpio, Leo, and Taurus.

The NWO does not have a government, but they have put a system in place through corporations.

They are attempting to put it in place also with the UN.

Their thought, what they are trying to implant, is that one religion will be easier to control than one world currency.

They call WIFI the "we fry you people." Rtintel is what your mobile is. They study you, what you do, and your habits and patterns. There will come a time when people will tear down all the towers, the electronics that are destroying the world. When you are in electronics, your brain goes "bye-bye."

There are still solutions though—prayers and meditations. Not for yourself, not for a special country, not for some political people or specific governments, but for the entire world to get involved. Not against terrorists or political events. But please, prayer for the peace, for love and compassion, for happiness of the entire planet, all the galaxy, and every human being. This is it. Do not pray for you before you pray for the entire world. This is the answer to the pollution, the wars, the terrorism, the MSG in the food, the chemicals in food and drink, the vaccination shots, the chemtrails, etc.

It is time that you all stop being angry to each other and be egoistic or jealous or judging each other. Or you will be left alone.

Put your aura in three layers. Gold, the rose sunset, blue or green. Put the cloak over. Be invisible and unnoticed. This is the end of the games.

People are going to wake up angry. They will not be able to think logically or reason. And it is what has been pushing people into immediate today. We are so close, we are in a massive change.

They want to stop the change you can make, and this is what has brought about by Harry Potter, for the most part.

Atlanteans are back using their gri-gri, manipulating and controlling human beings. The founder of Atlantis was in charge of crystal on earth, and he has laboratories.

But while most of the controlling extraterrestrials on this planet are malevolent, you have received the help of the Pleiadians, who are trying to help undo what the reptilians, Sirians, and malevolent Anunnaki have set up on this planet for you.

The current administrators of the empire government on the planet have a lineage back to Orion hybrid reptilians while the money was given to Marduk's children, the Rockefellers (Ra-Ka Pharaohs) and the Rothschilds. Marduk (mar (mr, son of) duk (dog Sirius). Marduk was identified with planet Mars.

Rockefellers and Rothschilds are both part of this consciousness.

The Teleporter Phone Booth

As a shaman and a visionary healer, VIE knows that the body is held by sound. In today's society, everybody has forgotten the ancient common wisdom of the link between our inner world and the outer world. Sound is note and notes are colors. The presence of disease indicated that the body has gone out of tune. Specific tones and irradiation of color light is necessary to connect and rebalance it to normal. DNA light radiation modulating certain frequency patterns unto light ray with it influences the DNA frequency and thus the genetic information itself. The process of hyper communication is most effective in a state of relaxation, free from stress and worries. Your DNA is a bridge between matter and the journey for those who seek to explore the multidimensional realms of time, space, and beyond—using multidimensional music, sound, and the language of the light to awaken your highest potential and defragmenting old programming and replacing it with the light and the sound of the "Now Divine Plan." Space will then be created to incorporate new harmonies in the body, healing it on all planes. Because the language of light is cosmic light intelligence, carried in color streams of consciousness, embracing the light and the sound of creation to expand consciousness with Bio-Qi Therapy™.

NEW CENTURY, NEW AGE, NEW EXPERIENCES

CHADD added its creation, a chamber with sound frequencies and music where clients can enter in during session. It is a very specific cylinder that changes the reality and from which people can enter in contact with another time in space.

But VIE entered that morning her private space and found herself standing in an old phone booth that teletransported her to a completely different time and space. From this booth, she found out that it is possible to destructively scans objects and transmit them through encrypted communications across any distance and rebuild it on the other side.

The object at one end of the system is milled down layer by layer, creating a scan per layer, which is then transmitted through an encrypted communication to a 3D printer. The printer then replicated the original object layer by layer, effectively teleporting the object from one place to another.

People are looking very healthy, and they have the choice to eat and breath or not. Most of them do not, and this is why they are in perfect shape and live around two thousand years old. They regularly go to generation chamber of light and sound, which is also a rejuvenation treatment.

The chamber of regeneration and rejuvenation where I astral projected several times is located in the vicinity of the Akasha. It is for souls that just need rejuvenation and regeneration. It is where souls that just graduated goes or newborn babies or the ones in the womb go. It is for people that are going to be incarnated or reincarnating.

Answers in Truth

CHADD has been taken away for nineteen months when I went to consult a third lawyer. I had some news from him, but the place was kept secret, and he did not know where he was, so he could not tell me. He could call me once a week for a few two to three minutes, but it was all. I had called Carolina, the social worker, but she refused to answer.

So I went to consult a third lawyer, recommended by a friend that time. I saw Mr. Marquez's face changing while looking at his computer screen. He finally looked at me embarrassed and said, "I am very sorry, but I do not see any case, and I cannot locate him anywhere. There is not even a case to defend. I have never seen such a thing in my entire career."

I replied, "But how come? It's impossible. He can't just vanish from the system." I called again Carolina, the social worker, and asked her again to tell me where he was and for answers

She laughed at me on the phone, saying, "No wonder he can't be located in the system," and she hung up.

For a week, I reflected, writing all sort of questions concerning my situation and the mission that CHADD and I carry as the chosen ones. Meditating every day for a few hours on the unreal things and events that were happening to us and the business. On the website, that I found out lately was created deliberately in such a way that it has never worked. The Chinese Thuggees that stole the Vajra and it for an exchange of service to Miguelito in the Philippines, Miguelito that knew that it was mine and had agreed to mail it back but kept it, trying to use it. The man working for the government paid to drive all over the state, delivering suspicious documents and packages, that took CHADD one day and forced him to visit a dealership to meet the mother of a young handicapped girl, who told him, instead of hello, "I have no panty under my dress." The pastor that sent the mafia to beat CHADD. The archon's son Paul that works for the government with the mafia and is doing human trafficking, all the different mental hospitals where CHADD was admitted, and I was sent to visit and document, etc.

I was in deep meditation when I felt an unknown energy approaching me and a very polite voice saying, "Dear Lady, I am the Honorable."

I heard him first making a prayer for me, which followed his teaching of the "Prayer of Demand."

"In the name of Jesus the Christ and the power that Jesus Christ has bestowed to me, hereby through the name of Jesus, I cast out all unclean spirits in me, on me, and attached to me in anyway. And in the name of Jesus, they will never return and reattach to me in any place and in anyway. In the name of Jesus Christ, so be it. Amen."

The Honorable came to clean my body from the unclean spirits the harsh women sent to me and my body.

Then I heard him turning very fast some pages, and he began to tell me this story of the creation of the feminine and masculine person and asked me if I could write about it.

Visions began to appear of the creation of the stories of Adam associated with the creation.

"The Babylonians because of immediate contact with the remnants of the civilization of the Adamites, enlarged and embellished the story of man's creation; they taught that he had descended directly from the gods. They held to an aristocratic origin for the race, which was incompatible with even the doctrine of creation out of clay.

The legend of the making of the world in six days was an afterthought, more than thirty thousand years afterward. The sudden appearance of the sun and moon may have taken origin in the traditions of the onetime sudden emergence of the world from a dense space cloud of minute matter, which had long obscured both sun and moon.

The story of the creation of the earth in six days was based on the tradition that Adam and Eve had spent just six days in their initial survey of the Garden. Adam's spending six days inspecting the Garden and formulating preliminary plans for organization was not prearranged; it was worked out from day to day. The choosing of the seventh day for worship was solely incidental to the facts herewith narrated.

Like the story of creating Eve out of Adam's rib is a confusion with the arrival and the celestial surgery connected with the interchange of living substances that is associated with the coming of the corporeal staff of the Planetary Prince more than 450 thousand years previously.

A great majority of the world's people have been influenced by the tradition that Adam and Eve had physical forms created for them upon their arrival on earth. The belief in man's having been created from clay was well-nigh universal in the Eastern Hemisphere; it can be traced from the Philippine Islands around the world to Africa. And many groups accepted this story of man's clay origin by some form of special creation in the place of the earlier beliefs in progressive creation evolution.

Adam and Eve arrived at midseason, when the Garden was in height of bloom. At high noon, the two seraphic transports, accompanied by Jerusem, personally entrusted with the transportation of the biological uplifters to earth, settled slowly to the surface of the revolving planet in the vicinity of the temple of the universal father.

All the work of rematerializing the bodies of Adam and Eve was carried on within the precincts of this newly created shrine. And from the time of their arrival, ten days passed before they were recreated in dual human form for presentation as the world's new rulers. Then they regained consciousness simultaneously. They are designed to work in pairs.

The planetary Adam and Eve were members of the senior corps of material sons on Jerusem. They belonged to the third physical series and were a little more than eight feet in height.

Mankind tended toward the belief in the gradual ascent of the human race. The fact of evolution is not a modern discovery, and the ancients understood the slow and evolutionary character of human progress. Although the various races of earth became sadly mixed up in their notions of evolution, nevertheless, the primitive tribes believed and taught that they were the descendants of various animals. Primitive people made a practice of selecting for their "totems" the animals of their supposed ancestry.

The Old Testament account of creation dates from long after the time of Moses. Moses never taught the Hebrews such a distorted story. He simply presented a condensed narrative of creation to the Israelites, hoping thereby to augment his appeal to worship the Creator, the Universal Father, whom he called the Lord God of Israel.

Moses in his early teachings did not attempt to go back of Adam's time, and since Moses was the supreme teacher of the Hebrews, the stories of Adam became intimately associated with those of creation. That the earlier traditions recognized pre-Adamite civilization is clearly shown by the fact that later editors, intending to eradicate all reference to human affairs before Adam's time, neglected to remove the tale reference to Cain's emigration to the Land of Nod, where he took himself a wife.

The Hebrews had no written language in general usage for a long time after they reached Palestine. They learned the use of an alphabet from the neighboring Philistines and did little writing until about 900 BC, and having no written language until such a late date, they had several different stories of creation in circulation, but after the Babylonian captivity, they inclined more toward accepting a modified Mesopotamian version.

Jewish tradition became crystallized about Moses, and because they endeavored to trace the lineage of Abraham back to Adam, the

Jews assumed that Adam was the first of all mankind. Yahweh was the creator, and since Adam was supposed to be the first man, he must have made the world just prior to making Adam. And then the tradition of Adam's six days got woven into the story, with the result that almost a thousand years after Moses's sojourn on earth the tradition of creation in six days was written out and subsequently credited to him.

When the Jewish priests returned to Jerusalem, they had already completed the writing of their narrative of the beginning of things. Soon they made claims that this recital was a recently discovered story of creation written by Moses. But the contemporary Hebrews of around 500 BC did not consider these writings to be divine revelations; they looked upon them much as later people regard mythological narratives.

This spurious document, reputed to be the teachings of Moses, was brought to the attention of Ptolemy, the Greek king of Egypt, who had it translated into Greek by a commission of seventy scholars for his new library at Alexandria. And so this account found its place among those writings, which subsequently became a part of the later collections of the "sacred scriptures" of the Hebrew and Christian religions. And through identification with these theological systems, such concepts for a long time profoundly influenced the philosophy of many Occidental people.

The Christian teachers perpetuated the belief in the fiat creation of the human race, and all this led directly to the formation of the hypothesis of a one-time golden age of utopian bliss and the theory of the fall of man or superman, which accounted for the nonutopian condition of society. These outlooks on life and man's place in the universe were at best discouraging since they were predicated upon a belief in retrogression rather than progression, as well as implying a vengeful deity, who had vented wrath upon the human race in retribution for the errors of certain one-time planetary administrators.

The 'golden age' is a myth, but Eden was a fact, and the Garden civilization was actually overthrown. Adam and Eve carried on in the Garden for 117 years when, through the impatience of Eve and the errors of judgment of Adam, they presumed to turn aside from the ordained way, speedily bringing disaster upon themselves and ruinous retardation upon the developmental progression of all Gaia.

Adam and Eve came to institute representative government in the place of monarchial, but they found no government worthy of the name of the whole earth. And before the collapse of the Edenic regime, he succeeded in establishing almost one hundred outlying trade and social centers where strong individuals ruled in his name. The sending of ambassadors from one tribe to another dates from Adam's time.

Adamson was the first born of the violet race of Gaia, followed by his sister and Eveson, the second of Adam and Eve. Eve was the mother of five children, three sons and two daughters, before the Melchizedeks left. The next two were twins. She bore sixty-three children, thirty-two daughters and thirty-one sons, before the default. When Adam and Eve left the Garden, their family consisted of four generations numbering 1,647 pure line descendants. They have forty-two children after leaving the Garden besides the two offspring of joint parentage with the mortal stock of earth.

Their children did not take animals' milk when she ceased to nurse the mother's breast at one-year-old. But Eve had access to a great variety of nuts milk and the juices of many fruits. She had full knowledge of the chemistry and the energy of those food, and she combined them to nourish her children until the appearance of their teeth.

There was no cooking in Adam's household. They ate once a day, shortly after noontime. Adam and Eve also imbibed 'light and energy' direct from certain space emanations in conjunction with the ministry of the tree of life. The body of Adam and Eve gave forth a shimmer of light, but they always wore clothing with the custom of their associates. Through wearing very little during the day, at eventide they donned night wraps. The origin of the halo encircling the heads of supposed pious and holy men dates back to the days of Adam and Eve since the light emanations of their heads was discernible. The descendants of Adamson always thus portrayed their concept of individuals believed to be extraordinary in spirit development.

Adam and Eve could communicate with each other and with their immediate children over a distance of about fifty miles.

This thought exchange was affected by means of the delicate gas chambers located in close proximity to their brain structures. By this mechanism, they could send and receive thought oscillations. But this power was instantly suspended upon the mind's surrender to the discord and disruption of evil.

Their children attended their own schools until they were sixteen, the younger being taught by the elder. The youngest changed activities every thirty minutes, the oldest every hour.

And it was certainly a new sight on Gaia to observe these children of Adam and Eve at play, joyous and exhilarating activity just for the sheer fun of it. The play and humor of the present-day races are largely derived from the Adamic stock. The Adamites all had a great appreciation of music as well as keen sense of humor.

At twenty, they were eligible for marriage, then began their lifework or entered upon special preparation therefor. The practice of some subsequent nations of permitting the royal families, supposedly descended from the gods, to marry brother to sister dates from the traditions of the Adamic offspring, mating as they must need with one another. The marriage ceremonies of the first and second generations of the Garden were always performed by Adam and Eve.

The children of Adam were trained intellectually until they were sixteen in accordance with the methods of the Jerusem schools. From sixteen to twenty, they were taught in the Gaia schools at the other end of the Garden, serving there also as teachers in the lower grades. The entire purpose of the western school system of the Garden was socialization, the afternoon periods to competitive play. The evenings were devoted to practical horticulture and agriculture, the afternoon to competitive play, and the evening to social intercourse and cultivation of personal friendships.

Religious and sexual training were regarded as a duty of parents.

The Adamites taught that 'Who so sheds man's blood by man shall his blood be shed, for in the image of God made he man.' Adam did his best to discourage the use of set prayers, teaching that effective prayer must be wholly individual and that it must be the desire of the soul. He taught the equality of the sexes."

The Honorable Man's Guidance

After having been guided by many from other realms—Catholic archbishops, monks, priests, suns, saints, Tibetans, aliens of different planets, and her star sister Anabelle—VIE has now entered in communication with the Honorable Man.

"Through all the incarnations, human beings have been persecuted again and again for the light. It must be shared with other people. Much wisdom and understanding will soon come to light. You've been in initiation with many beings. And now is the time to share. Everyone must have a clear idea of what is the earth that we like to call Gaia. It is a one-room school house where everyone learns at its own pace. No one learns lessons simultaneously. It began as a gigantic laboratory, and the truth has been hidden to you. You have been kept in legends and stories by the Custodial.

After birth, the main source of learning is through relationships and interaction with others. Through joy and pain is how a human being progress its spiritual paths. In relationships, emotions are invoked and you react. Sometimes a negative event may be the hand-opening door. It is only in community, in relationships, and only in service that you can truly understand the all-encompassing love. A life with difficulty, filled with obstacles, presents the most opportunity for the soul's growth. That is when the lessons are learned. Learn to forgive, learn to unlearn all negative traits including anger, hatred, violence, greed, pride, lust, selfishness, and prejudice.

It is important to learn to forgive from a difficult event but never forget lessons if you want to progress and go forward.

You have not given much support to the heart's frequency in your dimension. In truth, the high incidence of heart disease on your plane is a direct symptom of this, as with most other diseases. It is now imperative to turn the leadership over the heart and allow again the heart to rule rather than the mind.

Compassion is not an idea but an energy that creates great oscillations in the fabric of the universe. Gratitude is not a polite statement but an energetic acknowledgment to the universe that you are in alignment with the source. Love is not romantic or a religious exclamation but is quite profoundly the energy that powers all creation.

To create and manifest, you need joy and passion.

Come with me, breath in, relax, and allow the experience fully; it will assist you to enhance your pathway and help others as a mirror while you are traveling through space and time."

I found suddenly myself in front of a large translucid crystal dome of a beautiful, elegant, and fashionable design. As I got close to the entranceway, a tall beautiful angelic entity escorted me inside a vast building. Inside it contains many sections of various energies for numerous activities of the crystal dome. I crossed a long corridor, and as I walked the corridor, there was a great number of fountains and cascades of pure energy springing forth from various places.

Then I have been taken into a huge planetarium.

"This is why I am with you today," said the Honorable. I want you to have a clear view of all events of the past era on the earth and its inhabitants because we have entered the new Aquarius Era."

The planetarium made me travel through the history and events of the past on Gaia. All the following has been given to VIE telepathically:

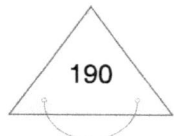

NEW CENTURY, NEW AGE, NEW EXPERIENCES

Ancient Mesopotamian tablets credit one God in particular with supervising the genetic manufacture of the *Homo sapiens*. That God was name Ea. Prince Ea known as Enki, which means "lord of earth." Ea was said to have lost his dominion over major portions of earth to his brother Enlil. Ea opposed many of the cruelties that other Custodial rulers, including his half-brother Enlil, inflicted upon human beings. Ea did not intend *Homo sapiens* to be harshly treated, but his wishes in that regard.

The Adam and Eve narrative is also derived from earlier Mesopotamian sources, which described life under Custodial "gods." The *God* or *Lord God* of the Bible's Adam and Eve story can therefore be translated to mean custodial rulers of earth. According to the Bible, Adam, who symbolizes first man, was created by God from the dust of the ground. This idea reflects the older Mesopotamian belief the *Homo sapiens* was partially created from clay. Adam's wife was also created artificially. In the name, biblical story of Adam and Eve, the *Homo sapiens*' attempt to obtain the knowledge they needed to escape their enslavement.

The Old Testament tells us that Adam was the first man and designed to be a servant. And there was one unpardonable sin that they must never commit: it is to never attempt to seek certain types of knowledge, symbolized in the story as two trees—the "tree of knowledge of good and evil" that symbolizes an understanding of ethics and justice and the "tree of life" that symbolizes the knowledge of how to regain and retain one's spiritual identity and immortality. A true understanding of ethics, integrity.

This was a highly effective way to deal with Adam's and Eve's rulers, intended to make humans live their entire lives and die without ever rising above the level of arduous material existence. In the story of Adam and Eve, we noted the appearance of a snake. The serpent was said to be God's enemy, Satan. The snake symbol had two very important meaning back then. It was associated with the Custodial god Ea, reputed creator and benefactor of mankind, and it also represented an influential organization with which Ea was associated.

The snake was the logo of a group that had become very influential in the early human societies of both hemispheres. This group was a disciplined brotherhood dedicated to the dissemination of spiritual knowledge and the attainment of spiritual freedom. This brotherhood was also known as the Brotherhood of the Serpent. They were opposed to enslavement of spiritual beings, and according to Egyptian writings, it sought to liberate the human race from custodial bondage.

Brotherhood teachings included physical through spiritual means, and the snake also came to symbolize physical healing. And it is featured on the American Medical Association logo. The snake became a venerated symbol to humans and an object of custodial hatred. Ea and his father, Anu, possessed profound ethical and spiritual knowledge. It was the same knowledge that was later symbolized as trees in the biblical Adam and Eve story. From the tree hang two pieces of fruit. To the right of the tree is a half-moon, the symbol of Ea, and to the left is the planet symbol of Anu. The drawing indicated that Ea and Anu were associated with the snake and its teaching. Ea, who was symbolized as a snake, was banished to earth and was extremely villainized by his opponents.

By creating a work race and the brotherhood of the snake, the god Ea had helped build a trap for billions of spiritual beings on earth. This corruption of the brotherhood, and the overwhelming effect it would have on human society, was already apparent by the year 2000 BC in ancient Egypt.

Mummified bodies—Ancient Egypt believed in a soul or self as an entity totally separated from the person's body and named such spiritual entity the *ka*. They believed that the ka, not the body, was a spiritual entity, and that the body itself had no intelligence or personality without a spiritual entity. And the Egyptians were made to believe that the spiritual well of the ka after death depended upon the ka maintaining contact with the body.

The derailment of spiritual knowledge in Egypt was caused by the corruption of the brotherhood of the snake, to which the pharaoh and the priests belonged. Brotherhood began to distort spiritual truth and perpetuate theological irrationality. The original uncorrupted brotherhood engaged in a pragmatic program of spiritual education. The organization's approach was scientific, not mystical or ceremonial. The subject of the spirit was considered to be knowledgeable as any science.

It seems that the brotherhood possessed a considerable body of accurate spiritual data, but it had not succeeded in developing a complete route to spiritual freedom prior to its defeat. The brotherhood's teachings were arranged as a step-by-step process. All pupils took oaths of secrecy in which they swore never to reveal the teaching of a level of any person who had not yet graduated up to that level. The teaching of the brotherhood in Ancient Egypt was organized into an institution known as the Mystical Schools.

The schools furnished the pharaohs and priests with most of their scientific, moral, and spiritual education. The first temple built for use by the mystery schools was erected by Pharaoh Cheops. Inside those temple walls, spiritual knowledge underwent deterioration, which caused pharaohs to mummify their bodies and bury wooden boats. The teachings of the mystery schools were created by the great teacher Ra, an important Custodial god.

The mystery schools not only twisted spiritual knowledge, they greatly restricted public access to any theological truth still surviving. Only the pharaohs, priests, and a few others worthy were accepted into the schools. Initiates outsiders, the "secret wisdom" they were taught, students were threatened with dire consequences if they broke the vow. Rosicrucian is one of the mystical systems that arose out of the brotherhood teachings.

Spiritual knowledge was severely limited. The biblical "revolving sword" preventing access to the "tree of knowledge" was being put into place by those who ran the mystery schools. The brotherhood's most famous offshoot: Christianity. Some brotherhood members in Egypt wore the same special outfits with a cord at the loin and a covering for the head, as later used by the Christian monks. The chief priest of the Egyptian temple wore the same type of broad-sleeved one used today by clergymen and choir singers. The chief priest also shaved his head in a small round spot at the top—an act later adopted by Christian friars.

History records that the Custodians used extraordinary violence to make *Homo sapiens* believe falsehood. Moses educated in Egypt became a high priest of the brotherhood under the reign of Pharaoh Amenhotep, or Akhenaten.

To the brotherhood, the most important mystical symbols were aprons. The brotherhood's mason guilds survived down through the centuries. Guild members were often free men and were therefore frequently referred to as Freemasons. The guilds of Freemasons gave birth to the mystical practice known today as Freemasonry. The mystical Freemasons became a major brotherhood offshoot that would take on great political importance later in history.

The priests of ancient Egypt wore similar aprons as a sign of their allegiance to the gods and as a badge of their authority. In Ancient Egypt, a statuette depicts an Egyptian prince holding his hands in a ritualistic posture that of the Rosicrucian Orders, described as familiar to all Rosicrucian lodge and chapter members. A prominent feature of the statuette is the triangular apron worn by the prince. During Egypt's first dynasty, the symbol of the apron and one of its associated mystical rituals came from that period of Egyptian history when the gods were said to be so literal that furnished homes were built and maintained for them.

Melchizedek presided over an elite branch of the brotherhood named after him: the BC, the Melchizedek Priesthood. Beginning around the year 2200, ceremonial aprons were made out of white lambskin. White lambskin was eventually adopted by the Freemasons who have used it for their aprons ever since. The brotherhood network was expanded throughout the entire Eastern Hemisphere by aggressive missionaries and conquerors. One of their targets became India.

The swastika is a very old emblem. It has appeared many times in history, usually in connection with brotherhood mysticism and in societies worshipping Custodial gods.

Jesus belonged to a Hebrew religion known as the Essenes. Joachim, Anna, and Mary were also members of Essene temples. Being Arian was a requirement to becoming an Essene; Jesus himself was white-skinned and redheaded. Essene order was accomplished only after several years' probation. The Essenes practiced initiation rituals in which they swore to never divulge their secret teachings. They also held confidential the names of the angels said to be living among the Essenes in their closed communities.

Christian missionaries made Jesus a household name and created a powerful new faction that would further divide human beings into battling groups. The successful effort to make Jesus the figurehead of a new Judgment Day religion about the most famous apocalyptic writing in the western world: the Revelation of Saint John. It leaves Christians with the same type of dire prophecy that the Hebrews had been left with at the end of the Old Testament: the coming of a great global catastrophe followed by a day of judgment.

Christianity began to change. The humanitarian foundation created by Jesus eroded as Christianity became more political.

The political transformation of Christianity got its first big push in the Western Roman Empire with the Christian conversion of its ruler, Constantine the Great.

The Crusades—The message given to Mohammed was a new religion called Islam. Members of Mohammed's faith are called Moslems, which come from the word *Muslim*, meaning one who submits. Islam was one more Custodial religion designed to instill abject obedience in human. The supreme being of the Islam faith is named Allah. Five hundred years after the death of Mohammed, the Christians launched a coordinated military effort to force the Moslems out of the Holy Land. This effort is known as the Crusades.

The Christian Crusades was to free Palestine from the Moslems. Minor battles between Christians and Moslems had broken out beforehand, but it was a call to arms by Pope Urban II on 1905 that finally turned those skirmishes into a paganized war effort involving nearly every Christian ruler of Europe. Not only were the crusaders killing Moslems, they were also killing Jews in Europe. A genocidal wave in the German Rhineland was the first major episode; it was sparked by unsubstantiated rumors that Rhineland Jews were using Christian children in their religions sacrifices. Obliterating the Jews became an important part of the Crusades, and the massacres continued even after the Crusades went to Jerusalem.

VIE

The Christian crusaders were led primarily by two powerful knight organizations with intimate brotherhood ties: the Knights Hospitaller and the Knights of the Temple (Knights Templar). Their purpose was aid and comfort. In the 1118, the Knights Hospitaller underwent a change of leader and purpose. They were made into a military order dedicated to fighting the Moslems who were continually trying to recapture Jerusalem.

They soon became affiliated with the brotherhood network by adopting brotherhood traditions and titles. They became ruled by a grand master and developed secret rites and rituals. By 1119, one year later, the Hospitallers had become a lighting order, the Templar Knights were in existence.

They originally called themselves the Order of the Poor Knights of Christ because they took solemn vows of poverty. Although the Templars and Hospitallers had a common enemy in the Moslems, the two Christian organizations became rivals.

They became the Knights of Malta, then changed to Knights of Rhodes when they moved to the island of Rhodes. While in Malta, the knights became a major military and naval power in the Mediterranean until they were defeated by Napoleon. The Knights of Malta had their headquarters moved to Rome under Pope Leo XIII. Today they are known as the Sovereign and Military Order of Malta. SMOM runs hospitals, clinics, and leper colonies throughout the world. It also gives active assistance to anticommunist causes and are surprisingly influential in political, business, and intelligence circles despite its small size.

By Philip IV (Philip the Fair) in France, the Templar controversy had become too strong, and he ordered the arrest of the Templars within the dominion and tortured them to extract confessions. Five years later, the Pope dissolved the Templar order by papal decree. Many Templars were executed, including Jacques de Molay, who was publicly burned in front of the cathedral of Notre Dame in Paris.

The Templar Knights organization managed to survive and was given a home in Portugal. They were granted their usual rights and privileges, wore the same costumes, and were governed by the same rules they had before. Templars change their name to Knights of

NEW CENTURY, NEW AGE, NEW EXPERIENCES

Christ and also changed the cross on their uniform from the Maltese cross to the official Latin cross.

To the list we can add two famous Christian orders, the Franciscans, which appeared to be quite human and adopted the cord-at-the-loins outfit and bold spot used by the Egyptian brotherhood priests, and the Dominicans that were placed in charge of the most widely hated of the Crusades: the Catholic Inquisition.

Pope Gregory IX placed them in charge of investigating the Albigenses. He gave them full power to name and condemn all surviving heretics. The church was no longer the humanitarian decentralized religion envisioned by Jesus. The new Catholic, "undivided" Church headquartered in Rome had succumbed to the reforms of the Eastern Roman Empire emperors. It was a religion Jesus would have deplored.

Looking at the spiritual practices of the Christian Knights and the Moslem Ismailians, we see that participation in warfare was often exalted as a spiritual quest. Warriors on both sides were inspired by corrupted brotherhood mysticisms, which taught that spiritual rewards could be earned by engaging in military endeavors against fellow human beings. This was the mythology of the spiritually noble war in gallant soldiers who were promised eternal salvation and a place in heaven for fighting a noble cause. This mythology still remains vital today for recruiting people to participate in continued warfare, twisting the urge for spiritual freedom into an honoring the war.

But if war helps to bring money, war is also institutionalization of criminality. Money itself is not valuable; the purpose of money is to facilitate the exchange of goods and services. Money is therefore an extension of war and cannot bring about spirituality improvement because criminality is one of the main causes of mental spiritual deterioration. Societies exalting in criminal actions will suffer rapid deterioration. Spiritual doctrines that combat are doctrines that degrade the human race.

The illuminati and Rosicrucians were major powers behind a new wave of religious movement. The Catholic Church had fallen into the hands of Pope Leo X, son of Lorenzo Di Medici, who was the head of a wealthy international banking house in Florence.

Under John XXIII, the Medicis were awarded the task of collecting taxes and tithes that were due to the Pope. The Medici operated a network of collectors to accomplish the undertaking. The Catholics believed in the importance of paying indulgences in money paid to compensate for their sins.

As a Catholic priest and educator, Martin Luther was subject to the strict regimen that was imposed to all clergy of the church and regular confession. At that time, confessionals were done improperly and Luther found it difficult. He felt compelled to seek another path, and he claimed that he was trying to reestablish the primitive Christian Church of Jesus. Another form of Christianity was born, and it only departed from the true teachings of Jesus. While Catholic teaching still had many flaws and lacked a true science of the spirit, these ideas reflected some of the truth and decency that were at the heart of Jesus's message. Luther said that the Pope was the forces of the Antichrist and it resulted in war between Catholic and Protestants, like today in Ireland.

The Protestant sects today account for around one-third of all Christians worldwide and nearly half of all Christians in North America. Luther's seal consisted of either side of two brotherhood symbols that are the rose and the cross, the chief symbols of the Rosicrucian Order. During his life and after, imported individuals and families who were active in the illuminati and in Rosicrucian supported Luther. One of them was the head of the powerful royal house of Hess, whose descendants would later held important positions in the brotherhood organization and in German Freemasonry.

Calvin teach his own interpretations of the Protestant doctrine resulting of a Protestant denomination named after him. They were forbidden to drunkenness, gambling, and dancing.

The Bank of England established the pattern for our modern central banks system, often led by the brotherhood. The purpose of a central bank was to put the government into debt so the government became the major creditor. Over twenty years after, France established an identical bank setup.

The Count of Saint Germaine was an agent of the brotherhood. He claimed to possess that alchemical elixir of life, immortality. And some claimed to have seen him after his death. His birth was a mystery, and he has been said that he was a human vampire and was raised by the Medici family of Italy. Roman Catholic and Freemasonry have both their origins in the brotherhood, and Louis XV issued an edict forbidding all French to have anything to do with the Freemasonry. With his death, Saint Germaine's status emerged; he was the highest representative of the brotherhood. And one of the Theosophical Society declared that he was one of the Hidden Masters of Tibet who secretly controlled the destiny of the world.

The Rothschilds made a fortune from various activities, and he capitalized on the many shortages during the French Revolution and wars. And the Rothschild family name became synonymous with wealth, power, and banking. The German lodges were Christian in nature, creating problems for Jews, like Rothschilds. In order to participate in the Freemasonry, special Jewish lodges were created like the Melchizedek lodges. Then due to apparently some UFO events, a new sect was born, the church of Jesus Christ of Latter Day Saints, known as the Mormons.

Scientific psychiatry has sadly become politicized, though the efforts to cure people of mental affliction are as old as history. One of the earliest centers of scientific psychiatry was born in Germany. By redefining the nature of thoughts, mental abnormal experimenters theorized the mental illness could be cured and treatments and drugs could remedy and cure the mental illness. From there arose a multibillion-dollar drug industry and the MK-Ultra program.

As this journey of events is completed, CHADD is about to be released from the Chateau Asylum. Nineteen months have passed, and the monthly "scam review" kept reporting his release with different excuses. The harsh woman, the surrogate, that claimed to be the police, the sheriffs, the CIA, FBI, and the government made a phone call just when they were going to release him. She wanted him in a halfway house to be able to get a part of his check in return. But the elite in power is bound to fail and the archon with it.

The day after the eclipse, I received a text from one client asking for help. She wrote, "Could the solar eclipse make me feel funny. I just woke up in a full blown anxiety attack. I feel very scattered and spacey. I also feel very heavy like I can barely keep my eyes open."

Ron also contacted me. He said that he was guided by an entity during the eclipse time to make the astrological chart of the actual president of the United States. It was about the eclipse affecting the world leaders to be understood, and he says, "I also went to a meditation for peace, balance, and harmony tonight. It was to send good energy into the world to counterbalance some of the challenging energy triggered by the eclipse."

The eclipse hitting the president ascendant and Mars is good for him. His voters have been silent since the election. But the eclipse will activate them now. They are going to be coming out one by one and in masses going against the negative news media and demonstrators. However, the negative affect of the eclipse on the president is the fact that it conjuncts the star Regulus, which creates in leaders and royal families. So he is divided by two different energies from the eclipse. He will be OK, but the critical media just will not stop attacking him for "anything" he says and does. My one concern was about the eclipse affecting the world leaders.

VIE placed her attention to the back of her head where the cerebellum is. Something then happened in her perspective. It is the back chakra that allows going from one universe to another. Human were capable of these capacities up to a certain time of the history till some strands of DNA were disconnected.

This was one of the many information that was shown to VIE in a scroll a light environment that are formed around all of the strategic points of peace and brotherhood in the world, inspiring the remnant of humanity to work with the higher intelligence.

The faithful were shown how a superior technology could intervene to save the world from total annihilation. How biological codes are controlled by gravitational fields and how biochemistry of life could be made to vibrate at any orbital level that is consistent with any spectrum of electromagnetic activity being used by the higher intelligence of the living light.

NEW CENTURY, NEW AGE, NEW EXPERIENCES

It was revealed to her how the brothers of light watch this and other planets go through cycles of experimentation for billions of years and how each planet goes through a great purification before the leap ahead. Many of the Watchmen are observing God's creation and operate from some energy platforms woven into the grid structures of gravitational matrices.

A new meridian of time then comes, and the foundations of the earth will be shifted to a new magnetic foundation as the orbit of the earth is reset within the ocean light.

VIE saw seekers of spiritual freedom and autonomy from power structures, building communities of love and light around the world. Using their souls and muscles to fashion healing centers of light and teaching centers where the love of God is preparing the young to use the spiritual gifts of creativity.

And she saw that the forces of spiritual opposition to the light washed away by the torrent of the Ancient of Days. This was followed by a victory song, sung by thousands of light beings proclaiming the triumph of YHWH's Legions of Light over the negative star systems that fought their orbits.

Then the bodies of light of righteous were preserved by the Lord Adonai's Son of Light and the Son covenant with the righteous in garment of protective light. And many of the righteous were removed from the earth through the command of Michael and Melchizedek.

The physical form of life passed into greater light, and the matter bodies of the faithful were advanced into the fifth dimensional bodies of light, into the greater universe.

Christ will come down from revolving light clouds with multitude of masters gathered around him. Many will be glad and many will be sorrowful at the sight for they did not recognize that their masters were in the midst, walking among the earth.

Is it fiction disclosing the reality? Is this real or is it fiction?

About the Author

VIE Loriot de Rouvray is a visionary healer, writer, musician of Bio Institute of Light and Sound Therapy, and has been recognized by Elite Women Worldwide for dedication, achievement, and leadership in her professional endeavors. She is an honored member of the National Association of Professional Women, honored member of the Continental Who's Who, honored member of the Worldwide Who's Who, recognized honored Strathmore's lifetime member, and is in the Hall of Fame of Best Alternative Holistic Medicine of Orlando. VIE is a member of Healing International.

VIE de Rouvray was born of the French aristocracy on an island called New Caledonia, which is located between Australia and New Zealand. In January 1987, VIE de Rouvray experienced a dramatic shift in consciousness, which resulted in a complete lifestyle change. Her purpose, which involves communication in the healing arts, was revealed, and gifts from previous interplanetary incarnations were activated. A visionary and an Aquarius, Ms. de Rouvray heals people metaphysically. She has also been guided to write and to create bio-music with the language of the light that she speaks.

VIE de Rouvray authored the book *911 Complete Guide to Natural Healing*. The book's purpose is to help achieve perfect health by utilizing holistic therapies, natural methods, and various other remedies. She discusses how other medications don't cure the body but unbalance even more your body, about vaccinations that contain mercury and are harmful to the body, and much more concerning your health that is hidden to the public.

VIE de Rouvray also authored the first volume of *Destiny of the doG*, a theory thriller about a journey of a tainted angel and about how the culmination of historical events will interact with the prophecies of the future days. The book features the ancient city of Antioch, fallen angels, ancient legends, and secret religious sect created in the days of Jesus. The book illustrates a modern adventure through which Christianity is introduced to the world.

VIE de Rouvray also wrote the book titled *Time is Ticking: The Fifth Amendment*. The second volume of this work explains the world today. It illustrates a fascinating and historical adventure that includes the return of Jesus and Mary Magdalene, who demonstrate the path of Divine love.

VIE de Rouvray wrote her third volume, *Window through the Window of Time: The Spiritual Journey of Two Angels*. It's about two angels at work. One is a physical light and vibration healer guided to be reconnected to her original essence, who is now here in a different life to see the transformation from the age of Pisces to the age of Aquarius. And the second angel is a Baker Acted, drugged ward of state that holds the key to Divine wisdom. It's the Armageddon and the last battle between good and evil, the final war between human governments and God.

VIE de Rouvray truly began her healing mission when she was reunited with her colleague who was in a wheelchair and wanted help. He was on psychotropic prescriptions drugs, hungry, anemic, blind, and in a constant foggy state of mind. VIE stopped seeing clients for four months so that she could focus all her time on him. He didn't have money and couldn't even drink or eat on his own. She nourished him, took care of him, and helped him detox from his medications, in spite of the fact that she could only communicate with him during a few moments of clarity throughout each day. Although caring for him was controversial to people who did not approve, Ms. de Rouvray never gave up. This was the first step of her mission.

VIE Loriot de Rouvray speaks the language of the light that is the galactic language of love and light. She tones, chant, and hand signs the language of the light that is instant communication with the infinite mind using pictographic cybernetics. It is the parent of the language of the Deity used in overall plan to design to outline a procedure, to code knowledge into crystal, etc., to reach many planetary worlds and realities simultaneously and fuse the different languages into the same scenario abstract. The universal language is light coded information to reawaken the DNA and the dormant aspect of your Divine blueprint. It carries encodements for frequency healing, activating DNA. It is used for healing any issue, for toning, meditating, aligning. Light language in short is a carrier of codes and vibrational frequencies of the fifth dimension, vibrating high enough to be able to channel light language.

She believes that spiritual growth, vitality, and wellness is the link to human primary purpose. In her eyes, life is a game, an adventure that has to be experienced, examined, and understood in order to restore balance in body, mind, and spirit. Ms. de Rouvray believes the end result of the infinite growth is to realize oneness, and thus the meaning of life is growth in consciousness through mental, physical, and mind experiences, like pain, stress, anger, fear, illnesses, and diseases.

She says that her purpose and intention as a visionary intuitive healer, spiritual and metaphysical teacher, and an Aquarius, she helps teach the body to heal at a deep cellular level, and it is designed to assist people to open their own self-healing ability and personal empowerment. She uses sacred geometry because sacred geometry transmits energy and awareness for soul awakening. Many frequencies of energy are very different in their qualities and purposes.

VIE

She created and owns the Biostimulation Institute of Light and Sound Therapy.

E-mail: instituteofbiostimulation@yahoo.com
Website: www.instituteoflightansound.com
Phone number: 407-902-7199
Twitter: www.twitter.com/Lightsound4
Facebook: www.facebook.com/BioInstituteOfLightAndSound
Video: Journey to the Fifth Dimension, Orlando
Young Living distributor number: #398498

Milton Keynes UK
Ingram Content Group UK Ltd.
UKHW020830190324
439596UK00007B/225